**Adventure House
Presents**

KA-ZAR
THE GREAT
June 1937

ISBN: 1-59798-126-5
ISBN-13: 978-1-59798-126-2

KA-ZAR
THE GREAT

Vol. 1, No. 3

CONTENTS

June, 1937, Issue

A Thrilling KA-ZAR Novel

PAGE

Ka-Zar The Great, powerful lord of the jungle, battles against the cunning and cruelty of the warriors of the Lost Empire and the heathen gods of that mysterious world.

Three Gripping Short Stories

Busted out of the service and seeking nothing but revenge Hicks gets a chance to prove he's a real man—the hard way.

The daring Americano with more nerve than caution wages a fight to the finish against the perils of Brazil.

On mysterious Papeete, the good deed that Don Prince once did for a native is returned with interest and when most needed.

ALL STORIES IN THIS MAGAZINE ARE NEW AND HAVE NEVER APPEARED IN PRINT BEFORE

Cover painting by
J. W. Scott
Illustration by
L. F. Bjorklund and
Earl Mayan

KA-ZAR, published bi-monthly by Manvis Publications, Inc. Office of Publication, 4600 Diversey Ave., Chicago, Ill. Editorial and executive offices, RKO Bldg.-Radio City, New York. Entered as second class matter, February 19, 1936, at the Post Office in Chicago, Ill., under Act of March 3, 1879. Entire contents copyright, 1937, by Manvis Publications, Inc. Manuscripts will be handled with care but no responsibility is assumed by this magazine for their safety. For advertising, address American Fiction Group, RKO Bldg.-Radio City, New York. Yearly subscription, $.50.

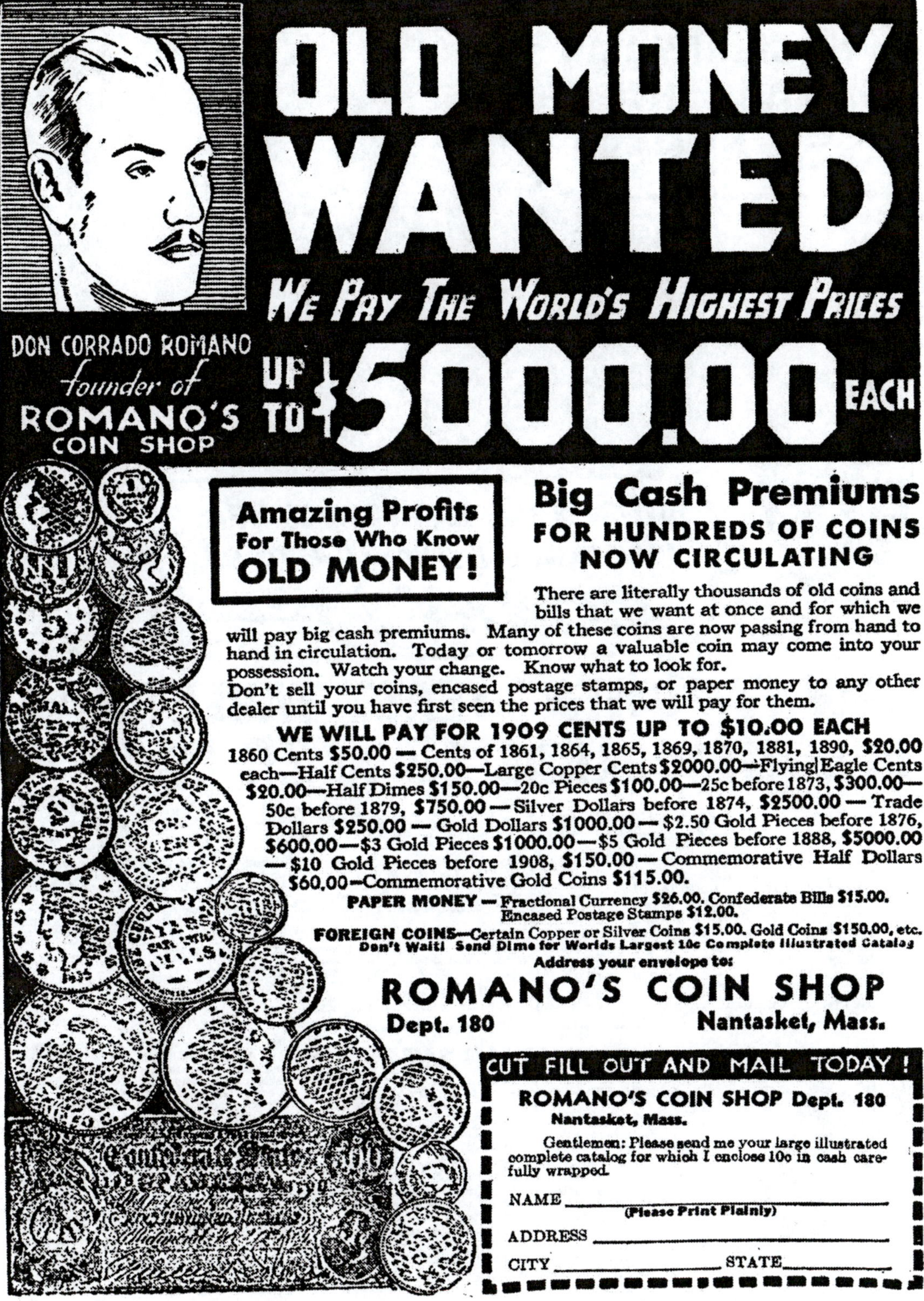
OLD MONEY WANTED
WE PAY THE WORLD'S HIGHEST PRICES
UP TO $5000.00 EACH
DON CORRADO ROMANO
founder of
ROMANO'S COIN SHOP

Amazing Profits For Those Who Know OLD MONEY!

Big Cash Premiums
FOR HUNDREDS OF COINS
NOW CIRCULATING

There are literally thousands of old coins and bills that we want at once and for which we will pay big cash premiums. Many of these coins are now passing from hand to hand in circulation. Today or tomorrow a valuable coin may come into your possession. Watch your change. Know what to look for.
Don't sell your coins, encased postage stamps, or paper money to any other dealer until you have first seen the prices that we will pay for them.

WE WILL PAY FOR 1909 CENTS UP TO $10.00 EACH
1860 Cents $50.00 — Cents of 1861, 1864, 1865, 1869, 1870, 1881, 1890, $20.00 each—Half Cents $250.00—Large Copper Cents $2000.00—Flying Eagle Cents $20.00—Half Dimes $150.00—20c Pieces $100.00—25c before 1873, $300.00— 50c before 1879, $750.00 — Silver Dollars before 1874, $2500.00 — Trade Dollars $250.00 — Gold Dollars $1000.00 — $2.50 Gold Pieces before 1876, $600.00—$3 Gold Pieces $1000.00—$5 Gold Pieces before 1888, $5000.00 — $10 Gold Pieces before 1908, $150.00 — Commemorative Half Dollars $60.00—Commemorative Gold Coins $115.00.

PAPER MONEY — Fractional Currency $26.00. Confederate Bills $15.00. Encased Postage Stamps $12.00.

FOREIGN COINS—Certain Copper or Silver Coins $15.00. Gold Coins $150.00, etc.
Don't Wait! Send Dime for Worlds Largest 10c Complete Illustrated Catalog
Address your envelope to:

ROMANO'S COIN SHOP
Dept. 180   Nantasket, Mass.

CUT FILL OUT AND MAIL TODAY!

ROMANO'S COIN SHOP Dept. 180
Nantasket, Mass.

Gentlemen: Please send me your large illustrated complete catalog for which I enclose 10c in cash carefully wrapped.

NAME
(Please Print Plainly)
ADDRESS
CITY   STATE

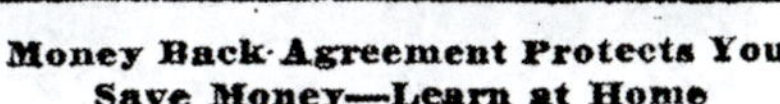

I Will Send You a Sample Lesson FREE

Clip the coupon and mail it. I will prove to you that I can train you at home in your spare time to be a RADIO EXPERT. I will send you my first lesson FREE. Examine it, read it, see how clear and easy it is to understand—how practical I make learning Radio at home. Then you will know why men without Radio or electrical experience have become Radio Experts and are earning more money than ever as a result of my Training.

Many Radio Experts Make $30, $50, $75 a Week

Radio broadcasting stations pay engineers, operators, station managers up to $5,000 a year. Spare time Radio set servicing pays as much as $200 to $500 a year—full time servicing work pays as much as $30, $50, $75 a week. Many Radio Experts own their own businesses. Manufacturers and jobbers employ testers, inspectors, foremen, engineers, servicemen, paying up to $6,000 a year. Automobile, police, aviation, commercial Radio, and loud speaker systems are newer fields offering good opportunities now and for the future. Television promises many good jobs soon. Men I have trained are holding good jobs in all these branches of Radio.

Many Make $5, $10, $15 a Week Extra in Spare Time While Learning

Starting the day you enroll, I send you Extra Money Job Sheets. They show you how to do Radio repair jobs that you can cash in on quickly—give you plans and ideas that have made good spare time money—from $200 to $500 a year—for hundreds of fellows. I send you Radio equipment to conduct experiments and give you practical Radio experience.

Money Back Agreement Protects You Save Money—Learn at Home

I am so sure that I can train you successfully that I agree in writing to refund every penny you pay me if you are not satisfied with my Lessons and Instruction Service when you finish. I'll send you a copy of this agreement with my Free Book.

Get My Lesson and 64-Page Book FREE. Mail Coupon

In addition to my Sample Lesson, I will send you my 64-page book "Rich Rewards in Radio," FREE to anyone over 16 years old. My book describes Radio's spare time and full time opportunities and those coming in television; describes my Training in Radio and Television; shows you actual letters from men I have trained, telling what they are doing and earning; tells about my Money Back Agreement. MAIL THE COUPON in an envelope, or paste it on a penny postcard.

J. E. Smith, President
National Radio Institute
Dept. 7DK1,   Washington, D. C.

OWNS PART TIME RADIO BUSINESS

"I am a locomotive engineer with the B. & M. Railroad, and work part time in Radio. In the selling end I have made as high as $300 in one month and have added to that about $100 in service work." FRANK McCLELLAN, 902 Elizabeth St., Mechanicville, N. Y.

PARTNER IN LARGE RADIO SUPPLY HOUSE

"Our concern has grown by leaps and bounds until it is today the largest wholesale Radio supply house in New England. We have established branches at Portland, Maine, and Barre, Vt. The N.R.I. Man travels the highway to profits in Radio." REYNOLDS W. SMITH, 1187-91 Elm Street, Manchester, N. H.

DOUBLED SALARY IN 5 MONTHS

"Shortly after I started the N.R.I. Course I began teaching Radio classes at the Spartan School of Aeronautics. After five months I was given a chance to join the American Airlines at a salary double that which I received from the school." A. T. BROTHERS, 2554 Hill St., Santa Monica, California.

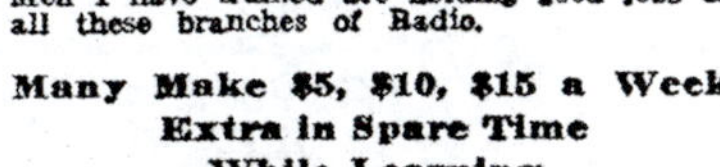

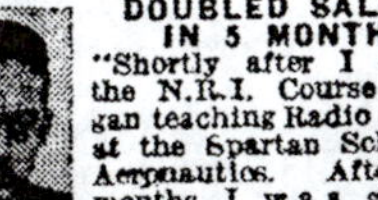

Thousands of Trained Electrical Men are making good money in the many branches of Electricity. Train for a better job—Right NOW!—whether you're 16 or 40. Look about you. Industry everywhere is being modernized with new electrical equipment—will use more ELECTRICITY. Many power plant operators now make up to $50 a week. Electrical Maintenance Men are paid $150 a month and up. Refrigeration and Air Conditioning Service Men earn $30—$40—$50 a week. Armature winders make $40 a week and more. Aviation Ignition Men also make good money at steady jobs. Many others operate their own business. These are only a few of the opportunities in Electricity.

COYNE extends the helping hand to YOU, too, if you're in a low-pay, discouraging job. Break out of the untrained class! If you are interested in bettering your place in life, get into ELECTRICITY—the gigantic growing field that employs more men than any other industry on earth!

Train on FULL SIZE Equipment—
NOT by Correspondence—NOT by Text Books

COYNE Shop Training is NOT by correspondence or Home Study. You come right to the big COYNE Shops in Chicago to get this practical Training. You work on real equipment—such as generators, real dynamos, you wind armatures, work on diesel engines, airplane motors, and do many other practical Electrical jobs. Here is one of the greatest working outlays of its kind in America. No embarrassing reciting. No dry text books. You don't need high school education or previous experience. It is this real job Training that enables COYNE to train you for a better pay job.

AIR CONDITIONING, DIESEL and
ELECTRIC REFRIGERATION included

Spreading over the nation is a vast network, these fast developing branches of ELECTRICITY are employing more men and paying more in salaries every year. Homes, offices, factories, trains, autos, airplanes are being air-conditioned. Autos may soon be diesel-powered. Instruction in these courses included without extra cost.

YOU TRAIN HERE
Many thousands of dollars worth of real practical equipment and machinery is installed in our fireproof modern school.

Many shop views like this shown in my catalog

Send for EASY PAYMENT PLAN
—New Low Cost Board and Room Plan

My friend, don't waste the golden years of your life saying, "I can't afford Specialized Training!" Of course you can! Get my catalog—see for yourself how we help graduates year after year. I have a special new low cost Board and Room Plan whereby students take care of their living expenses while at COYNE. Get training first, then pay tuition in 18 easy, monthly payments, starting 5 months after you begin school. So don't let lack of money keep you from sending this coupon for full details of my amazing plans!

PART TIME EMPLOYMENT

If you need part time work to help pay living expenses while here, we'll help you. We help hundreds of students through this special department and may be able to help you.

JOB AFTER GRADUATION SERVICE

We keep in touch with many large firms in many branches of ELECTRICITY, ready at all times to supply their needs for trained men. After you graduate you get Lifetime job assistance through our Free Employment Department. As a COYNE graduate you get free business service and technical consultation to help you as you advance in your job; also, the privilege of review at any time without additional tuition charge.

Employers PRAISE These COYNE Graduates

GET FULL FACTS
You'll see everything in the Big FREE COYNE Book . . . . facts...opportunities...jobs... salaries...actual photos of hundreds of ambitious fellows preparing for better jobs. You'll see proof that COYNE training pays. This big Book is yours without obligation. So act at once. Just mail Coupon.

"Mr. Lingerfelt's services very satisfactory. His practical shop training at COYNE has certainly helped increase his efficiency."

"John Lindquist was given an increase in salary due to the high quality of his work."

(Names of companies on request). We have scores of such letters. Get complete story. You owe it to yourself. Clip and send Coupon—NOW!

MAIL THIS NOW
for MONEY MAKING DETAILS

H. C. Lewis, President,
COYNE ELECTRICAL SCHOOL;
500 S. Paulina St., Dept. 47-15, Chicago, Ill.
Without obligating me, send full details and your Big FREE Illustrated Catalog.

Name............................Age..........
Street....................................
Town....................................State...........
Mail in Envelope or paste on Postcard

COYNE ELECTRICAL SCHOOL
H. C. LEWIS, President
500 S. Paulina Street   Dept. 47-15   Chicago, Illinois

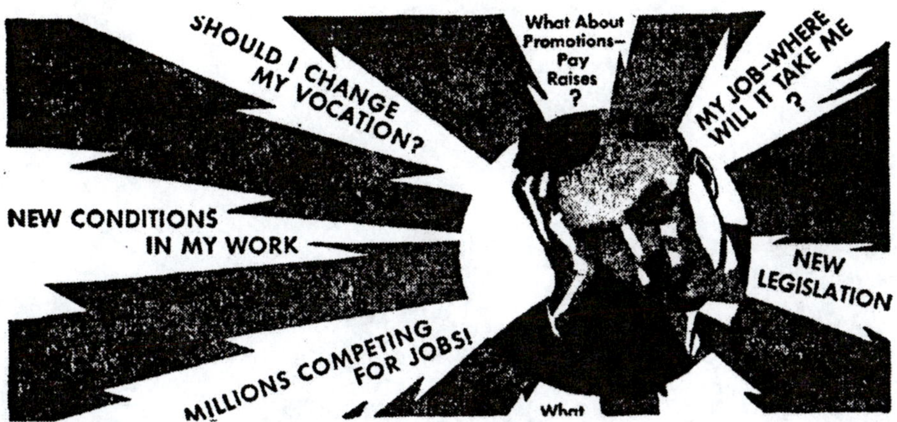

WHERE DO YOU GO FROM HERE?

YOU'RE like a million other men—you're facing a *big* question. The depression turned business topsy-turvy and now the rebuilding period stares you in the face.

Are the things that are happening today going to help or hinder you—what will they mean in your pay check? Where will they put you five, ten, twenty years from now? How can you take full advantage of this period of opportunity?

We believe you will find the answer here—a suggestion the soundness of which can be proven to you as it has been to thousands of other men.

The whole trend today—legislation, spirit, action—is to put men back to work, raise earning and spending power, *give every man a fair chance to work out his own salvation.*

The road to success remains unchanged but, bear this in mind, *what it takes to win is radically different!*

No employer today would dare risk an important post in the hands of a man who had not learned the lesson of '29. Why should he, when right at this moment he can pick and choose and get almost any man he wants at his own price?

Business organizations are rebuilding—reorganizing for the new conditions. Before it is over every man and every method will be judged in the cold light of reason and experience—then dropped, remade or retained. This spells real opportunity for the man who can meet the test—but heaven help the man who still tries to meet today's problems from yesterday's standpoint! Out of the multitude still jobless there are sure to be many frantically eager to prove him wrong and take his place.

Some Men Have Found the Answer

Seeing these danger signs, many aggressive men and women are quietly training at home—are wisely building themselves for more efficient service to their employers.

You naturally ask, "Has your training helped men withstand conditions of the last few years?"

Our answer is to point to a file of letters from many of our students reporting *pay raises and promotions while business was at its lowest ebb*—together with a myriad of others telling of greater success during these recent months of recovery.

Amazing evidence is ready for your investigation. We have assembled much of it in a booklet that is yours for the asking, along with a new and vitally interesting pamphlet on your business field.

This is a serious study of the possibilities and opportunities in that field. It is certain to contain an answer to vital questions bothering you today about your own work and earning power.

Send for these booklets—coupon brings them free. Be sure to check the LaSalle training that interests you most. We will tell you also how you can meet and take fullest advantage of today's situation. No cost or obligation—so why not mail the coupon now?

LASALLE EXTENSION UNIVERSITY Dept. 492-R, Chicago

Please send me—without cost or obligation—full information about how I can, through your training, equip myself for the new problems and opportunities in the business field I have checked.

☐ Higher Accountancy ☐ Business Management
☐ Law: Degree of LL.B. ☐ Traffic Management
☐ Commercial Law ☐ Business Correspondence
☐ Industrial Management ☐ Business English
☐ Stenotypy ☐ Salesmanship
☐ Modern Foremanship ☐ Office Management

Name ....

Position ....

Address ....

LaSalle Extension University

Zar, the lion, struggled to escape the landslide that he had created, dug in deep with his claws as with an ominous rumble the whole face of the bank came crashing downward.

The Lost Empire

Thrilling adventures of Kazar the Great

by BOB BYRD

CHAPTER I

THE ABYSS

RICH, abundant, overflowing with life, yes. Yet, that dark and impenetrable corner of the globe known as the Belgian Congo, is cruel. It is the land where the inexorable Law of Claw and Fang still reigns supreme. In fact, it is the only Law. Let the strong survive; let the weak beware lest they perish from the face of the earth. For the jungle knows no pity and mercy is dealt out only in swift death. There in the heart of a primeval wilderness, the price of life is eternal watchfulness.

Cruel, yes, is this steaming, miasmic jungle world. But there, hard on the equator, even more cruel is the brassy face of the sun as it shines from the vast dome of heaven at high noon.

So intense are its rays that they can fell an ordinary mortal in a matter of minutes. When the sun crosses its zenith, the heart of Darkest Africa stops beating. The lizard buries himself in the mud, the hyena slinks in his noisome den and no bird sings.

The unconquerable white youth, KA-ZAR THE GREAT, stalks his fierce enemies in a hidden empire of intrigue.

High noon. The earth lay panting. Yet from behind the matted screen of the jungle wall came unmistakable sounds of movement; the scarlet leaves of the shubah bush trembled, yet no breeze had stirred.

Who was this—man or beast—that came down the jungle trail in open defiance of the molten sun overhead? What dire necessity, what restless soul urged him on beneath the leaden weight of the sun?

Before the thrust of a massive gray head, the tangled wall of the jungle parted. Trajah the elephant, wise and venerable leader of his herd, moved slowly into the clearing. But Trajah was not leading his pack of cows and young bulls on one of their far-flung pilgrimages. Behind him came a far more strange and awe-inspiring procession.

Stepping where Trajah had stepped, came Zar the lion—Zar the Mighty, with regal head and saber-tipped talons. Clinging precariously to his ruffed mane, was a grimacing, ring-tail monkey.

But that was not all. Stranger still, more startling yet was the figure that brought up the rear of the procession—the figure of a man. He was naked save for a scant loin cloth around his middle. Tall like a God, proportioned like a Viking, his muscles rippled and flowed like tempered steel beneath his bronzed skin as he moved.

More arresting than his superb body, however, was his head. It was massive, leonine, topped by a thick shock of black hair that fell down to his shoulders. And out of his face stared two eyes, cold, alert—all-seeing, tawny eyes —that gave him a strange kinship to the lion who stalked before him.

Thus came Ka-Zar, Brother of the Zar the Mighty, at high noon.

Whence did he come? From his jungle domain many moon's journey behind him. Where was he going? Ka-Zar could not have said. He only knew that a strange restlessness was upon him—a restlessness so compelling that it even urged him on during heat of mid-day.

As he moved forward across the clearing, his mind went groping back over the years.

He did not know, of course, that many years before, John Rand, a prosperous mine owner from Johannesburg, had started out from that city in an airplane, taking his young wife and infant son, David, to Cairo. He did not know that the ship had crashed, to land in the heart of the Congo. A benevolent Providence had wiped out the memory of those first nightmare days and nights in the jungle.

Now, twenty years later, vague and disturbing memories of his beautiful and adored mother rose up to haunt him. Her tragic death, before the onslaught of a mysterious jungle fever, had been mercifully obliterated by time.

Ka-Zar's first clear recollections of his boyhood were those of happy days roaming the wilderness with his father. He did not know—and he would never know—that on the day before he and his father were to start on the long trek back to civilization, John Rand had been struck by a falling tree; that as a result of that accident, his father's mind had become unbalanced.

From that time on, the course of young David's life was changed.

To Rand's warped mind, the lonely grave of his wife in that God-forsaken stretch of wilderness, became a sanctuary. And all the miles of dense forest, of clearing and river and lake surrounding it, became his and David's —to hold sacred and inviolate against any trespasser.

The trespasser had come—in the shape of an evil and greedy white man and his native helpers. Keeping his fanatical trust, attempting to drive the newcomer from his wilderness domain, John Rand had been slain. And young David, left alone, had come into his kingdom.

A true child of the wilderness, David had early made friends with the beasts. On one occasion he had saved Zar the lion, mighty lord of the jungle, from a treacherous bed of quicksand. And in his own hour of need, when his father died in his arms from a murderer's bullet, Zar did not forsake him. The watchful lord of the jungle, had stood guard by the grief stricken boy and had led him at last to his own jungle lair.

There a pact of brotherhood had been sworn. There the boy ceased to be David Rand and be came instead Ka-Zar, brother of Zar the lion. There he learned to speak the language of his brothers, the beasts. And there, aided by his superior intellect and the few weapons he had learned to fashion and to use, he had earned the right to rule over his vast heritage.

Years later the evil white man—the slayer of his father—had returned and Ka-Zar, fulfilling a vow made over the graves of his parents, had avenged the death of his father. He had learned many things in that encounter. He had learned to respect the white man's weapons; to mistrust the white man for his greed, his cruelty, his treachery.

And later, he had learned to his sorrow, to distrust the white man's mate— woman. Especially one, the laughing, blue-eyed, golden haired girl, Claudette.

Since that day, two long rainy seasons ago, when he had said his last farewell to her, he had known no peace.

Claudette had betrayed him; or so he thought.* He had sent her away forever, without a backward glance. He well knew that leagues without measure separated him from her, yet the bitterness of it was, that she was forever in his heart. In every pool of water he saw her laughing face and blue eyes. No gazelle bounded across his path but he saw her tantalizing figure dancing before his eyes.

And it was to flee from her—though in his heart he knew there was no escape —it was to flee from himself and the memories that haunted him, that Ka-Zar roamed farther and ever farther away from his domain at high noon.

Half way across the clearing, Nono the monkey squirmed around on the lion's back and with one long, agile leap sprang to Ka-Zar's shoulder. Wrapping one spidery arm around his master's neck, he pointed the other towards the end of the glade where a growth of luscious green grass marked a water hole. He showed his teeth in a simian grimace and chattered vivaciously.

Ka-Zar pulled at the monkey's left ear with a rough affection. "Enough, silly one," he said with mock severity. "If you find the trail too hard, return to your long-tailed brothers and gossip all day in the tree tops."

Nono suddenly became absorbed in a burr that had caught in a tangle of Ka-Zar's hair and forgot what he had originally pointed out.

After one brief glance behind, Trajah, still in the lead, continued on across the glade. He, too, would have liked to have wallowed in a pool of cool water but his two-legged friend was driven

---

*See "Roar of the Jungle" Book 2 of the Adventures of Ka-Zar.

on by a force greater than himself.

Trajah was old and very wise. He had battled through a hundred mating seasons and in his shrewd animal brain he understood the thing that gnawed at Ka-Zar's heart. He was in search of . . .

Abruptly, without warning, the earth beneath Trajah's massive feet began to tremble. A second later there came a sinister, omnious growl from deep down in the bowels of the earth. Instinctively, with a squeal of warning, the huge, gray beast spurted forward.

AND as he charged, the earth that appeared so stable a moment before crumbled and melted away behind him. There was a sustained, cataclysmic roar, an enveloping cloud of dust as a thousand tons of earth sank from view.

By one short step, Trajah had managed to reach solid land. It was fifty yards, however, before he could check his charge and turn. Slowly, cautiously, his huge ears flapping and his trunk upraised he made his way back, testing the ground carefully at each step.

He approached the abyss far closer than was wise, considering his weight. The cloud of dust still hung over it and from far below came the last rumble of the falling earth. Slowly, as he waited with puzzled, worried eyes, the cloud of dust thinned out. And there, where Ka-Zar, Zar and the monkey had been but a minute before, was naught but a yawning hole in the ground.

In his long life Trajah had had experience with an occasional land-slide in the season of heavy rains but this was something beyond understanding.

A vague uneasiness possessed him. It was clear that his friends had disappeared down that yawning chasm. How deep was it? He edged forward cautiously but as the earth began to slip again beneath his tremendous weight, he lunged swiftly back again.

For once Trajah's greatest asset, his bulk, became a distinct handicap. It prevented him from edging close to the lip of the chasm. Helpless, confronted for once with a situation he did not know how to meet, he flung back his wrinkled trunk and gave vent to the trumpeting call of the bull elephant. The shrill note echoed and re-echoed throughout the jungle but from the bottom of the pit came no answering call.

Again and again Trajah split the silence with his clarion call until the very leaves trembled on the trees. No answer. After each challenge it seemed that a pall of silence fell over the world, more brooding than the one before.

All through that long, hot afternoon, the faithful Trajah hovered near the rim of the chasm, sending forth his call at regular intervals. He felt sure that if Zar or Ka-Zar were still alive, they would have answered him at once. The heavy silence that greeted his straining ears could mean but one thing.

The two-legged lion-man who had brought peace and justice to the jungle was dead—dead along with his brother the lion and the chattering monk.

Trajah knew that sooner or later, death comes to all things that live in the jungle. Yet a great sadness filled his heart. He would miss the two-legged one, whose delight it had been to ride upon his broad back. At sunset he trumpeted his call for the last time, then looked up and searched the heavens.

On a spread of pinioned wings, Kru the buzzard—the inevitable end of every jungle tragedy—was wheeling down to investigate.

Slowly Trajah went to spread the dire tidings throughout Ka-Zar's domain.

CHAPTER II

Signs of the Oman

BUT Kru was not to feast that day!

When the rumbling cave-in precipitated Ka-Zar and his friends deep into the bowels of the earth, Zar was the only one of the trio who did not lose consciousness. A spitting, whirling fury, he was enveloped by the deluge, tumbled over and over by the rush of sand, earth and stone. Buried completely, instinctively he fought for his life. Choking, gasping, he clawed desperately to escape his tomb.

His paws were raw and his lungs were filled with suffocating dust when at last his muzzle broke through the debris. Pausing only long enough to inhale deeply of damp air, he wormed his tawny body free.

Far overhead was a distant patch of blue sky—the gaping hole in the earth's crust through which they had fallen. It seemed to Zar that he stood in some strange kind of a cave, but the light was too dim to see far in any direction. Near him he could make out the tiny form of Nono, piteous and motionless huddle of fur. But the monkey was not Zar's chief concern. The great lion swung his shaggy head about and peered into the Stygian gloom for his brother.

But Ka-Zar was not to be seen. He was buried—somewhere under that pile of earth and sand. With a low whine of anguish issuing from his throat, Zar sniffed the staggering mound. Whether he detected the faintest of faint scents or whether by sheer instinct, he paused before a certain spot of loose sand. Then, with his worn and bleeding claws he began frantically to dig.

Never had the jungle trio been closer to death—if death had not already struck. Never had they been in such strange and repelling surroundings. They were creatures of the open, of shady forest paths and of sun-bathed clearings; of emerald trees and sparkling streams. Here was a place of perpetual gloom; of dank, foul air; of silence broken only by the hushed drip of water.

The nearest that Zar's stout heart could know of fear, was the uneasiness which now possessed him. It was more than faith and loyalty that spurred him on. Nono was a silly, helpless creature —Zar needed his courageous and wise two-legged brother to stand by his side in the emergency.

If he was not already dead—Ka-Zar must not die!

It was in reality a matter of moments. But in that place of eternal twilight and eerie silence it seemed eons before Zar's torn paws flung back a last shower of earth and exposed a patch of bronzed skin. And it seemed centuries more before at last the unconscious giant had been dragged from his tomb—unconscious but still breathing faintly.

Dazed whimpering. Nono crawled over and squatted at his master's feet.

Ka-Zar's return to consciousness was a slow and painful process. His head throbbed; his mouth was hot and dry; his lungs were a torture. With an effort he struggled up to a sitting position and looked around him. Every inch of his body had been battered by the heavy earth and the rocks that had swept him downward. He was a welter of livid bruises, of torn and bleeding flesh.

Slowly his brain cleared. He heard Zar's low growl of relief, saw the huge lion tenderly licking his torn paws and guessed what had happened.

"My brother has saved me," he acknowledged simply, in the guttural language of the beasts.

Zar looked significantly about him. "Zar has need of his brother," he answered.

Nono crept forward, climbed up on Ka-Zar's shoulder, wrapped both arms about his neck and whimpered. Twinges of pain wracked Ka-Zar's body as he rose to his feet but a hasty examination soon told him that by some miracle, no bones had been broken in his perilous fall. Wistfully he looked up at the patch of sky, so hopelessly remote above him.

If he but had Pindar's wings. . . .

IN vain his eyes searched the sides of the shaft that led up to the light and life. They were sheer walls of rock— not even Nono could have attempted to scale them. By some evil mischance the trio had traveled over a treacherously thin crust of earth that had waited like a trap to snare them.

Trajah had been in the lead. It had been his tremendous weight that had started the cave in, and they in the rear had had no chance to escape.

Reluctantly he lowered his eyes and gazed about his prison instead. And as he became accustomed to the semi-darkness, he saw that it was not the small pit he had first imagined it to be. On three sides were rocky walls, down which water dripped steadily and monotonously. He walked over to the nearest, put one hand against the damp surface. Then his eyes flicked upward.

Just above the level of his head, strange marks had been scratched in the smooth face of the stone. Ka-Zar drew in his breath with a sibilant hiss. His eyes narrowed and he leaned forward to study the mysterious signs more closely. He made out a crude but unmistakable representation of the sun; several others were surely meant to be beasts; others still held no meaning for him. With a puzzled frown he turned to Zar.

"Others have been in this place before us," he explained in a series of low growls and grunts. "Omen—two-legged creatures like Ka-Zar."

At the mention of men, Nono

squeaked and tightened his grip around the jungle giant's neck. The long hairs on back of the lion's neck rose and bristled, his slitted eyes gleamed and the tip of his tail twitched, omen—in the language of the jungle, the name that meant men. A name to be conjured with, and dreaded. At first, instinct alone had warned the beasts to mistrust those strange two-legged creatures. Later, experience had proven the dire import of the warning.

Men had brought swift death and cruel suffering in their wake. The creatures of the forest had learned to hate and fear them—to hate their blood lust and their greed, to fear their sly and treacherous cunning.

Ka-Zar alone, ruler of the jungle, was the exception. And he, himself, though he had met good men and bad, had renounced them. He had learned to be wary of strangers, be they black men or white. And now as he stood irresolute in the subterranean chasm, he reminded himself that even though he walked upon two legs, in heart and soul he was a beast—the sworn brother of the mighty Zar and the ruler of the jungle creatures. Man, then, was his natural enemy, also.

It was with a strange mixture of emotions that he studied the curious hieroglyphics upon the dank wall. A thousand wild speculations crowded through his brain. The Omen who had scratched those marks—did they still exist? Or were they long dead and forgotten? Neither beast nor jungle native had mentioned this mysterious underground cavern. Where had these Omen come from? Who were they? Where had they gone?

Grimly Ka-Zar told himself that he would soon find out. To stay where he was meant a slow and agonizing death by starvation. With Zar at his side he must set out into the unknown and together they would face whatever might befall them.

Turning his back on the walls, he faced the vista of gray dimness that stretched out before him. His jaw was set at a hard angle as he called to Zar. "Come!"

The little monkey chattered with fright as he strode with long, purposeful steps into the dank twilight.

"Hush, silly one," warned Ka-Zar. "You may betray us with your chatter."

Zar fell into place beside him, suspiciously sniffing the air, feeling the earthen floor with every padded step. Ka-Zar fingered the keen knife that still dangled in its sheath at his belt, and thought longingly of the stout bow and the quiver of arrows that were buried deep somewhere in the landslide. It was futile to look for them he knew, for even if he could find them, they were undoubtedly shattered and useless.

NOW from ahead there came to their ears the subdued roar of rushing water. Their progress became slow and cautious for as they moved further away from the hole high up on the earth's surface, the light below grew dimmer.

A draft of air came up the tunnel through which they moved, touched Ka-Zar's cheeks with chill, damp fingers. And then around a sharp turn in the tunnel, they came at last to the source of the roaring—a swift-flowing, dark, subterranean river. Here they paused to bathe their bleeding wounds and to clear their dust-choked throats with drafts of the icy waters.

Somewhat refreshed, they resumed their cautious advance. The bank of the river was slippery footing. In places the stream was wide and its dark surface gleamed unbroken like a black mirror. In others it narrowed sharply and tumbled frothing over rocks and boulders in its bed. Once Ka-Zar stumbled over something and paused to examine what had tripped him. In the gloom, his sensitive fingers told him as much as his eyes. He picked up the object and turned it over and over in his hands. It was a vase of clay—he had seen similar objects in the kraals of the jungle black men.

Again his mind was haunted by wild speculations as to what danger lay before him and his friends. Small wonder that he found this underground passage a place of deepest mystery. He did not know it, but the most courageous explorer in the world would have known a touch of fear in the place; the most erudite scientist would have been baffled there. For Africa is the Dark Continent and the Congo is the Heart of Darkness. And here in the depths of the Congo lay things more fantastic than any civilized man had ever dreamed.

Several times Zar growled deep in his majestic throat, telling that this subterranean world of gloom was not to his liking. Each time Ka-Zar stilled him with a guttural warning. Nono had long since subsided into shivering misery.

Twice something swooped down over their heads, brushed noiselessly by with only a sudden rush of air to tell of its passage. Then far ahead they saw that the dimness of the tunnel was lightened by a flickering, reddish glow.

They turned the corner of an abrupt bend in the passage and saw, set in the wall ahead of them, a burning torch. Now their vigilance was redoubled. Their eyes peered ahead, past the spluttering beacon. Ka-Zar saw that the stream they had been following grew wider. Several times his fingers crept to the haft of the knife at his belt. But still the silence was unbroken. Nothing moved; nothing stirred. Shrewdly he guessed that long hours had passed since he and his friends had been swept down by the treacherous cave-in. It was now night and if by any chance there were Omen in the vicinity, they would probably be sleeping.

With a last warning for silence, he moved forward. His stomach muscles were drawn in, his belly was empty and he was hungry. Somewhere, somehow, they must find food.

CHAPTER III

The Temple of Pthos

A SHORT few minutes later they rounded a last bend and halted in amazement. The river widened out abruptly before them into a vast lake. From its shores the walls of the tunnel leaped upward in vaulted arches, tier upon receding tier, until they were lost in utter blackness. Here and there on the high parapets, like evil eyes in the blackness, other torches had been set into the rocky walls. And at their feet the tongues of flame were reflected eerily in the dark, still waters of the lake.

Straight ahead, far distant across the water, gleamed a steady pillar of flame. It was different in several respects from the sputtering tongues of the torches. For one thing it rose from an elevation higher than any. And its light was a pure, pale glow. Its very distance and the surrounding gloom made it seem detached, as though it floated in space.

Suddenly Zar's ruff rose. A quiver ran down the length of his huge, tawny form. His lips pulled back from his bared fangs and he snarled.

"Still!" warned Ka-Zar in a low voice.

He, too, had caught it—the faint but unmistakable scent of man! From slitted, tawny eyes he surveyed the black and silent lake and the towering cliffs hanging over it. Along the rocky walls his keen eyes made out many oblong patches of black shadow and his jungle instinct told him that they were the entrances to caves. As far as he could see, the cliffs were honeycombed with them.

His jaw tightened. Then he shrugged his massive, naked shoulders. Where there were Omen, there also was food. The thought whetted his already keen appetite. He turned and started off at a swift but silent stride, following the shore of the lake.

The hated scent of man grew stronger in his nostrils. And soon he came to the first shadowy opening in the bare face of the cliff. Peering into it, he saw a long, narrow tunnel leading into the rock. Another torch illumined its length.

Zar fell in behind him as he entered the passage. Soundlessly they traversed its length and at the far end, found that it branched off into two opposite directions. There was nothing to indicate what might lay at the end of either.

Ka-Zar detached the clinging monkey, dropped him lightly to the ground and then stooping over, laid his lips close to Zar's ear. "Go with Nono," he ordered in a low, hoarse whisper. "Ka-Zar goes the other way. Go silently—seek food, not trouble. Ka-Zar will meet his brother here at this spot later."

With a subdued growl to show that he understood, Zar turned into the left hand passage and glided off like a monstrous tawny shadow. The fearful Nono scampered nervously in his wake. Ka-Zar watched them a moment, then turned off to his right and with equal stealth moved off in the opposite direction.

He soon found that he had entered a veritable labyrinth. Here in the cliff, the narrow tunnels crossed and recrossed each other in a tangled maze. He halted in dismay and wondered if Zar, too, had been lost in a similar tangle. But there was nothing for it now. Of one thing he was certain. Men— many men—his traditional enemy, were here. And he did not relish the prospect of meeting them with a hungry, gnawing stomach.

One lead was as good as another. He turned off down the nearest shaft. In many places he had to stoop to clear the low rocky ceiling. It terminated in an elaborate, bronze door.

Ka-Zar halted before it, surprised. He studied the closed portal for a moment. Two straight pillars flanked it on either side. They were decorated with vividly colored paintings that made no sense to him. Some were of two-legged creatures whose heads were those of Nono the monkey or Nyassa the fish. Others had bodies of Sinassa the snake and the wings of Kru the vulture.

WITH every sense alert, with every nerve on trigger edge, he tried the door. To his surprise, it opened easily, swung noiselessly inward under the steady pressure of his shoulder. With one hand near his belt, he glided across the threshold, let the door swing back into place behind him.

After the low ceiling of the narrow tunnel, he was not prepared for the vastness of the chamber he had entered. Nor had the bare rocky passage prepared him for the dazzling splendor that now greeted his eyes.

Around him the walls rose high and sheer, decorated by pillars far more resplendent than those that flanked the doorway outside. Here were more vivid paintings, but these were augmented by embellishments of gleaming metals and twinkling gems. Before him a flight of steps, polished until they shone, led up to a broad dais. On either side of the platform were slender columns topped by glowing braziers. Blue smoke curled up from these, drifted down to him heavy with the pungent scent of incense. And between the two columns, in the center of the dais, stood the most repelling, the most amazing, object that he had ever seen.

Around its massive base many lamps burned with a strange, bluish light. It rose sheer, towering, threatening—an enormous figure that was far more grotesque than any of the painted representations on the walls.

Ka-Zar had seen the pot-bellied figures of clay that the jungle blacks worshipped as gods. But it took him a few moments to realize that this enormous figure before him was also a god. He walked slowly forward, studied it curiously. He saw a squat, misshapen body that was grotesquely human. Claw-like hands were folded across the swollen belly. The head of a hideous monster, with empty sockets for eyes and curved horns jutting from its low forehead, leered down at him.

Ka-Zar had no knowledge of history nor of religions. His clear eyes saw in that repulsive face all the greed and lust and cruelty of the Omen. And he sensed that men who would worship such a god must have hearts as black as the darkness in which they lived.

He forgot what he had come seeking. He was obsessed suddenly by a yearning for the brilliant sunshine of the world above, for the luxuriant green growth of the forest, for the familiar sounds of insects and birds and beasts.

But it was no sound that roused him suddenly from his nostalgic reverie. It was but a feeling—a vague warning that was born in his own brain—that made him suddenly tense and wary. He knew, without knowing why, that he was not alone. The flesh at the nape of his neck crawled where the gaze of invisible eyes rested upon him.

His nostrils flared a trifle and from slitted tawny eyes he searched the vaulted chamber. Slowly, very slowly he turned to face the door through which he had come. Then his gaze was irresistibly drawn upward. He stiffened as his own eyes met a pair of greenish orbs that glared malevolently back at him.

On a narrow ledge above the doorway crouched a sinister ebony form. Ka-Zar stiffened to rigid immobility as he recognized N'Jagi, black cousin of N'Jaga the leopard. Around N'Jagi's sleek throat was a slender collar of gold, studded with gems. His long tail switched. He lay flat on his belly, his ears back—the hideous guardian of this unholy temple. And Ka-Zar knew that if he took one step toward the portal, a spitting, clawing black death would descend upon him.

Only one beast had ever dared to challenge Ka-Zar's supremacy in the jungle. N'Jaga, the magnificent spotted terror of the forest, had dared to defy the might of Ka-Zar and his mighty brother Zar the lion. The feud had been a long and bitter one; a feud that would never die as long as the leopard tribe roamed the earth. In the final test, when N'Jaga and Ka-Zar had met in fair battle, N'Jaga had died by the jungle giant's hand.

NOW here was N'Jagi, far more treacherous, far more powerful, far more cruel than his spotted cousin. The black hate mirrored in his gleaming eyes was a challenge, a reminder to Ka-Zar that he was the ruler of the jungle and all its people. He rose to it. Flinging back his mane of long dark hair, he straddled his legs and faced his hereditary enemy—a magnificent figure, arrogant and commanding. Then with a reckless disdain for whatever men or beasts dwelled in that place, he expanded his mighty chest and sent the stentorian roar of the lion echoing and re-echoing through the temple.

The crouching N'Jagi heard and understood. Never before had the black leopard known fear. The two-legged creatures who dwelled deep in the earth had always trembled in terror before his baleful glare. Only one of them dared to approach him—and between him and this Om was a bond of black deviltry, a strange brotherhood of evil. Now this strange two-legged creature dared to defy him! He spat, but in his heart of hearts he knew a strange apprehension.

It angered him. He lashed his tail. A whining snarl issued from his throat. And then the two-legged one spoke to him in the language of the beasts.

"Spring, N'Jagi!" came the defiant taunt. "Spring at Ka-Zar—brother of the mighty Zar—and die!"

The glow from the braziers was reflected in the shining steel that leaped with lightning swiftness into Ka-Zar's hand. Still N'Jagi hesitated, glaring in impotent hate from his slitted emerald eyes. A blind lust to slay possessed him. He gathered his powerful muscles and his lips curled back from gleaming fangs.

"N'Jagi waits," called up Ka-Zar scornfully. "He is wiser than his cousin N'Jaga. For N'Jaga died by Ka-Zar's bare hands."

At the words, the smouldering fury in N'Jagi's heart burst into searing flame. His arrogant soul would admit of no master. His crafty brain urged him to back down, to bide his time and wait for vengeance. But the challenge of the jungle is not lightly ignored. There is no word for mercy in the language of the beasts. The weak are killed and the strong survive. And an enemy is forever an enemy until he is slain. Torn between the urge to destroy this bold two-legged creature and

this strange apprehension that had come for the first time to trouble him, N'Jagi wriggled uneasily on the ledge.

Ka-Zar waited no longer. Grasping his knife, with another guttural taunt he stepped deliberately forward. One step. Two steps. Three steps. . . .

Two more strides would carry him to the door. N'Jagi's fury overmastered his caution. With a hideous scream, his terrible claws spreading out into glistening steel hooks, he sprang.

Ka-Zar leaped nimbly aside as the shrieking black fury descended upon him. The fetid breath of the leopard was rank in his nostrils as the beast hurtled down beside him. The malevolent hate in the green orbs—a hate heightened by the knowledge that his first lunge had missed—was a living thing.

Then, before he could recover—before he could rip Ka-Zar from throat to loin with a slash of his saber claws— the jungle man leaped into action. And the jungle man was quicker, more sure and deadly than the leopard had been. With his shoulder he smote N'Jagi's shoulder, throwing the leopard back on his haunches. Then his left hand flashed out, knotted in an iron fist around the collar of gold that encircled the black cat's throat.

In his right hand the blade of his knife glinted brightly for a moment, then descended in a swift arc.

N'Jagi saw the blow even as it fell. Using his two hind legs as levers, he lunged violently to avoid it, at the same time lashing out with his fore-paws. Five streaks of liquid fire seared their way across Ka-Zar's chest as the leopard's claws drew blood. But his grip on the collar never loosened.

The blade descended, driving home through the satiny skin of N'Jagi's throat. Hot blood spurted up to Ka-Zar's hand. The leopard's eyes were glowing coals of pain and hate. He lunged again, slashed futilely with his claws at the empty air——then slumped in Ka-Zar's grip.

WITH a long, drawn-out breath the pent-up air escaped from Ka-Zar's lungs. Still holding up the limp body of the leopard by the golden collar around his throat, he disdainfully wiped his knife against the satiny hide, jammed it home into its sheath again. Then with a guttural snarl he cast the body from him.

As if the arrogant gesture had been a signal the massive bronze door swung open. The temple became a bedlam of shrieking shouts and cries and the rush of many naked feet. Ka-Zar whirled, his chin fell on his chest and his shoulders hunched. His knife flashed up again——but ere it could descend a horde of naked black men had thrown themselves upon him.

The dagger was clawed from his fist. Thumbs gouged his eyes; teeth sank into his flesh. By sheer weight of numbers the blacks overwhelmed him, sent him crashing to the floor of the temple beneath a pile of sweating, stinking bodies.

Even the mighty giant of the jungle was no match for such a horde. And after the brief but furious melee, when Ka-Zar was jerked roughly to his feet, he was truly a prisoner. Around his neck the blacks had slipped a collar of copper, to which was attached a heavy chain.

Dazed, sick at heart, trembling with impotent fury he straddled his legs and glared at his captors. As the reddish film dissolved gradually from his eyes, he saw them clearly for the first time. They were black, true, but strangely different from the jungle creatures he had known. These men were puny, their arms and legs spindly and misshapen. Instead of glistening ebony, generations of living deep under the ground had turned their skins to a dull, unhealthy-looking gray. Their eyes were sunken deep in the sockets of their skulls and they wore only ragged and filthy loin-cloths. They jabbered excitedly to one another in a tongue that he could not understand.

Like a lion at bay surrounded by a pack of mangy dogs, Ka-Zar stood in their midst. Though he could not understand their talk or the gibes they spat at him, their expressions were easily readable. Their lacklustre eyes mirrored at the same time a cold fury against the violator of the temple and a superstitious awe as they saw the lifeless body of the black leopard.

Ka-Zar faced them without fear. That the fate which awaited him was probably a dire one, he did not care. It was the feel of the collar about his neck that revolted his very soul. The symbol of bondage——about the neck of the mighty Ka-Zar——King of the Jungle——brother of Zar the lion! It was unthinkable!

The chain clinked as he flung back his magnificent head, squared his massive shoulders and once more set the temple throbbing to the challenging roar of the lion.

CHAPTER IV

THE QUEEN CONDEMNS

THE first wan light of dawn was breaking over the Congo when in another temple, not far distant, a radically different scene was transpiring. Here the walls and the vaulted ceiling were of purest white. In the center of the tiled floor was a sunken pool. Papyrus plants fringed its edges and enormous lotus buds floated upon the still water.

Set in a vast niche in one wall was

the towering statue of a goddess. Her countenance was at the same time benevolent and yet stern; implacable and yet merciful. Her blank eyes looked down at the figure of a young girl who lay prostrate on the tiled floor at her feet.

The girl raised her head, lifted her arms in supplication. She was hauntingly beautiful. Beneath straight brows her eyes were deep pools of darkness. Her nose was finely chiseled and her mouth was a splash of vivid scarlet. Her slender body was exquisitely formed and of the rare tint of old ivory. A slender gold circlet in the form of a twisted snake bound her forehead and beneath it her hair fell to her shoulders, sleek, blue-black.

From a jeweled girdle that encircled her hips hung a sheath of some gossamer stuff. Above the girdle her ivory tinted body was nude save for cup-shaped discs of gold, that upheld her firm young breasts.

Her scarlet lips parted and aloud she communed with her deity in the strange language that had puzzled Ka-Zar.

"O all-seeing and all-powerful Isis," she began in a low, husky chant, "deign to aid thy troubled daughter. Remember in thy wisdom that when my forefathers fled their beloved Egypt the most precious burden of their blacks was thy image."

There was deep sorrow in her whisper as she continued: "Now my father the king lies buried beneath the temple. Times are troublesome in Khalli and my people are restless. O Isis, aid the proud Queen Tamiris who kneels so humbly before thee. Counsel me—guide me!"

The last faint whispers of her voice died away into silence as she prostrated herself once more on the tiles. For a long time no sound broke the stillness. If the goddess spoke words of wisdom, they were voiced only in the heart of the kneeling girl.

She rose at last. Her head came up and with a regal gesture of command, she clapped her palms sharply together.

Instantly the door to an ante-chamber opened and eight girls garbed in filmy white draperies—the vestal virgins of the goddess—glided into the temple. Some bore urns of incense, others huge fans of peacock feathers. One carried tame doves upon her arms and shoulders. As they approached, the humility Tamiris had displayed before the goddess dropped from her like a discarded mantle. She held her head imperiously high, her eyes flashed brightly and her lips were set in a straight, uncompromising line.

The priestesses fell into place about her and to the accompaniment of a melancholy, minor-keyed chant, Queen Tamiris walked slowly from the temple.

Already the first hot rays of the sun were slanting over the Congo. The high circular wall of unscaleable cliffs was shaded from deep purple at the base to a pale turquoise at the summit.

Jungle, lush and vividly green as Ka-Zar knew and loved it, covered the floor of the lost valley. On the far side of it, visible over the tree-tops, rising tier upon tier of sun-baked clay and stone stood the fabulous lost city of Khalli.

From its summit, pale now in the light of day, rose a steady pillar of flame. It was this eternal light that Ka-Zar had seen through a break in the cliffs the night before, when he had stood in the tunnel and looked out across the underground lake.

TAMIRIS' royal visit to the Temple of Isis was an occasion of state. It was a sumptuous procession that awaited her as she emerged from the building. Stepping into her gilded palanquin she sank back against its silken cushions and the conveyance was raised to the shoulders of four black slaves. The sun gleamed on fluttering banners and brazen trumpets as she was carried in regal style towards the distant city.

As the column traversed a broad path along the shaded floor of the jungle, the beauty of the Queen's face was marred by a dark frown. True daughter of the Ptolemies, she was quick to anger—slow to forgive; and she was more proud than Lucifer, himself.

She mourned her father now that he was dead, yet living, she had secretly despised him for his weakness. A keen child she had long guessed that the wise and crafty Zut was the real ruler of Khalli. And now, though she was still hardly more than a child, she vowed that Zut's reign was ended. For long years she had brooded in secret upon the matter and now that the time had come, she was determined to assert her own dominance.

The fringe of jungle thinned and from narrowed eyes Tamiris surveyed her fantastic kingdom. It was a strange city indeed that had grown up here in the depths of the Congo—an imposing pile that pyramided upward in flights of hewn stone steps, of terraces and hanging gardens, of palaces and hovels, of obelisks and market-places and tombs.

The procession began the long climb up the steps. The palanquin lurched as the leading slave stumbled, throwing Tamiris back against the cushions. Instantly her face flamed a dull crimson with rage. Thrusting her head from the side of the conveyance she addressed the trembling culprit.

"For that you shall have twenty lashes, clumsy one!"

The unhappy slave bowed his head and plodded on. Somewhat mollified, Tamiris allowed her mind to brood once more upon the tangled affairs of state.

When at last she dismounted before the vast portal of her magnificent palace, a breathless black emerged from the building, prostrated himself panting at her feet.

"Speak," ordered Tamiris coldly. "What do you wish with your Queen?"

"Daughter of the Sun," murmured the slave, "Zut desires your presence in the courtyard of the palace. There are those who wish audience with you."

Tamiris drew herself to the full of her diminutive height. Twin spots of color flamed in her smooth ivory cheeks. So Zut dared to summon her thus? The time had come to throw down the gauntlet and defy him. Let this slave tell him. . . .

She bit her under lip, changed her mind. No. Better to wait until she was in the audience hall. Let the multitude hear her challenge this usurping schemer. She made a gesture to the slave.

"Go. Tell Zut that the Queen comes."

Dismissing her cortege, Tamiris entered the building. At every step of the way guards saluted her with upraised spears, men and women of the household made obeisance as she passed. She walked past them, unseeing, unhearing, oblivious to their presence. Crossing a long hall, she found Zut waiting her near a door that gave out onto the main courtyard of the palace.

She surveyed him with ill-concealed hostility as he bowed gravely. A yellow robe was wrapped about his tall, cadaverous figure, his bare feet were shod with sandals made of thongs of leather. His sole adornment was a ring that held a monstrous moonstone, that looked out of place on his thin, claw-like hand. An unprepossessing figure, until one looked at his face.

ZUT was ageless. As long as Tamiris could remember his skin had always looked like wrinkled, yellow parchment. His loose and pendulous lips were hidden by a straggly beard. It was his eyes that were noteworthy, that held the gaze with an hypnotic fascination. Beneath jutting brows, set close on either side of a hooked and predatory nose, they were small but piercing. There was something of the power, the cunning and the cruelty of a bird of prey about this crafty statesman.

It was the Queen who spoke first. "You have requested my presence," she said coldly. "See to it that your reason for doing so is sufficient to warrant such presumption."

Zut allowed his lashless lids to droop over his eyes, veiling whatever expression her arrogant words might have brought to their depths. "It is a matter of the greatest import," he replied. "The Daughter of the Sun knows that trouble is brewing in Khalli. Through the long centuries the black slaves who dwell in the catacombs have multiplied, while the descendants of their masters, here in Khalli, steadily decline. The blacks realize the power of their numbers. They grow avaricious and resentful. Revolt simmers below the surface even now."

Tamiris squared her slim shoulders. "Let them revolt, if they dare. Every traitor shall die."

Zut shook his head, combed his beard with skinny fingers. "Spoken like a Ptolemy, Queen Tamiris. But such words must be backed with swords and with warriors. Thus far, only my persuasion with Seti, the High Priest of Pthos, has kept the embers of rebellion from bursting into flame."

Though she would not admit it, Tamiris knew only too well that what Zut said of the blacks was true. When her forefathers had fled down from Egypt with a handful of slaves, they had stumbled by accident into one of the natural tunnels that ran through these cliffs. A cataclysmic earthquake had sealed the passage behind them and doomed forever to live in this place, they had builded the city of Khalli in the little valley of jungle. Here the nobles had maintained, as well as they could, the culture and the arts of their native land.

But time and again slaves had fled and taken refuge in the caves that honeycombed the cliffs surrounding the underground lake. There in eternal twilight they had multiplied in number and degenerated in body and soul. Forswearing the goddess Isis they had set up a temple to the evil Pthos and rumors of obscene orgies and sacrifices drifted out to the city.

Now these worshipers of darkness had become a decided menace to Khalli and its inhabitants. The devil could rule them but not Tamiris the Queen.

All this passed through Tamiris' mind, but to Zut she said only: "Your reason for summoning me—what is it?"

Zut opened the door that led to the courtyard and as they stepped through onto a broad terrace, he explained: "The dwellers in the catacombs have captured an outlandish prisoner. Whence he came from, no one knows. They claim he has desecrated the temple of Pthos and they clamor for his blood. You can see for yourself what manner of man is this creature."

Tamiris walked to the edge of the terrace, looked out over the courtyard. It was filled from one end to the other with a milling throng of blacks, who sullenly and reluctantly prostrated themselves as she appeared before them.

Standing in their midst, bruised, battered but still magnificently defiant, Ka-Zar towered above them. Despite the hateful fetters about his neck he was still untamed, still the monarch of the jungle.

The daughter of the Ptolemies surveyed him with interest. No sculptor in Khalli could have modeled such a superb head, such a massive, muscular body in bronze. An instinct as old as Eve, but something which she did not as yet understand, stirred in the breast of the youthful Queen.

ONE of the blacks jerked at the chain fastened to the collar about Ka-Zar's neck. Ka-Zar glared at him and a low growl rumbled deep in his mighty throat.

"You see?" said Zut in Tamiris' ear. "He speaks no language, but growls and snarls like a beast. He is naked, save for the skin of an animal about his loins."

"Yet," retorted Tamiris, "he is worth ten of Khalli's best warriors—and worth a hundred of these puny slaves."

Zut rubbed the side of his hooked nose with a bony knuckle. "Perhaps. But the blacks demand his death. And the daughter of the Sun would be wise to placate them."

Without reply, Tamiris turned her back to him and walked majestically down the steps of the terrace. Placate these grotesque, malformed creatures who dared to question her sovereignty? Never! She would defy them, here and now. Defy Zut, also. How this jungle giant had managed to appear mysteriously in her domain did not matter, at the moment. Had it suited her purpose to toss his life away, she would have done it without a second's hesitation. But as a pawn in the game, he would be spared.

She walked up to Ka-Zar, came to a halt before him. All eyes in the courtyard were upon her, all ears waited for her to speak. Her scarlet lips parted—the multitude would soon hear her momentous challenge!

But she had reckoned without Ka-Zar. With powerful arms folded across his bronzed chest, he stared at the slight figure confronting him. For long months he had been tormented by the vision of a girl who he believed had betrayed him. To his simple soul, then, woman meant treachery and his hate had grown to include them all. That in itself was reason enough for him to feel instant antagonism for the exotic creature who now stood before him.

But that was not all. Despite his hatred, Ka-Zar had never been able to rid himself of a yearning for the golden-haired vision of his dreams. Claudette of the laughing face and eyes as blue as the skies after rain. Now he looked upon the face of Tamiris and her flaming beauty was an affront. It was a mockery—the fact that she should remind him of Claudette. For her eyes were hard and as brilliant as jet; her scarlet lips were set in a thin, straight line. And her lithe body was that of a jungle cat ready to spring.

Ka-Zar did not stop to analyze such complex emotions. In his simple heart he knew only that the sight of this exotic Queen was hateful to him. And he expressed that hostility in the natural way for him to do so. He distended his nostrils. A guttural, animal snarl rumbled in his throat. Then with a contemptuous gesture he tossed back his regal head and clenching his huge fists, he loosed from his lips the rumbling bass challenge before which the very jungle had always trembled.

A wail of terror rose from the blacks as they fell back. Their hands brandished the varied assortment of weapons they bore. Only Tamiris held her ground. She did not flinch; she did not stir. But there was no mistaking the defiance, the disdain, that this jungle giant was directing at her.

A pulse beat dully in the ivory column of the Queen's throat. Twin spots of angry color flamed in her cheeks. A violent rage, the heritage of her arrogant ancestors, possessed her. This naked savage—this—this jungle animal—dared to mock her!

With the roar of the lion, Ka-Zar had swept the carefully planned chessboard of diplomacy into a heap. Tamiris forgot that this creature was but a pawn in her royal game, forgot that a moment before she had been about to speak the word that would set him free.

In a torrent of the staccato, corrupted Egyptian that was her language, she showered the dire curses of the gods upon his untamed head. Ka-Zar listened and watched in scornful silence as she denounced him. His judgment of her was vindicated—in her flashing eyes, in her twisted lips, in the tiny hands that clenched and unclenched at her sides—she was every inch feline, cruel, savage.

Suddenly she straightened, raised one hand in an imperious gesture and spoke a swift sentence to the surrounding blacks. A concerted yell of triumph welled from their throats as they closed in about their prisoner. Then without a backward glance Tamiris turned, majestically ascended the terrace and disappeared inside the palace.

CHAPTER V

The Queen Retreats

WILLING hands pulled savagely as the chain attached to the collar encircling Ka-Zar's throat. Leaping and howling the blacks dragged him swiftly across the flag-paved courtyard toward the base of a massive monolith. It was fantastically carved in bas relief with more of the strange creatures that were neither bird nor man nor beast, but fantastic combinations of the three. Ka-Zar could see that encircling the monolith, head high, were a series of massive bronze rings.

He soon learned what they were for. A last painful jerk of the chain and one end of the linked halter that held him was slipped through one of the rings and cunningly secured.

He was chained—truly chained.

All his old hatred of the Omen swept through his heart. He had experienced nothing but sorrow and trouble at the hands of man. The first had slain his father—and in time he had died. The second had brought untold woe to his jungle domain—and he, too, had died. The third—the golden-haired girl. . . .

Bah! It was a raven-haired she-devil who held him enslaved now. Not with a laugh and a caress of soft hands —but with chains.

With a bitter snarl of resentment, Ka-Zar relaxed. Head on his chest, he brooded on his fate. The black-eyed she-devil had condemned him and if he could have understood her last words, he would doubtless know also the manner in which he was to die.

With pleased grins now, the blacks hovered about him. All through that day, with the broiling sun of the Congo beating down upon his head, he stood immovable, unblinking, chained to the monolith. The black men came to taunt him, to spit upon him, to lash him with gibes in their outlandish tongue. To Ka-Zar, brother of the mighty lion, they were but a pack of mangy hyenas—he ignored them all.

Their vile words he could not understand and they hurt him not. The occasional spear with which they prodded him, or the stones they flung, were but indignities and irritations beneath his notice. His contempt was magnificent.

Only once did his amber eyes flash fire, only once did the lion's growl rumble in his throat. One of the blacks approached him, a broad grin showing the sharp points of filed teeth. In his two hands he held a small urn out of which the water spilled as he walked.

He held out the vessel invitingly but as Ka-Zar reached eagerly for it, he let it slip from his hands to crash to the flags of the courtyard. It shattered into a thousand bits and the precious fluid trickled away across the sun-baked stones.

A fiendish howl of derision went up from the encircling blacks at the incident. Ka-Zar understood then that he had been tricked. His eyes smouldered. He lunged forward suddenly to the full length of his chain. Like a piston his long right leg flashed out and the toes of his bare foot, hard as granite, caught the culprit under the chin.

The black hurtled backward, crashed into three of his fellows and brought them down with him in his fall.

The jeers of the others gave way to a gnashing of teeth. Once more Ka-Zar fell back into his stoic calm. He regretted his wrathful outburst. Never again would these jackals arouse him from his superior indifference.

Thirst! He knew its tortures. First it made man or beast mad—then it destroyed them. Was that the fate that awaited him? Again he reflected on the wanton cruelty of man. The beasts of the jungle slay—slay for food. But the refinements of torture, of prolonged agony before the release of death—that was the product of the cruel, twisted brain of man alone.

He must conserve his strength. His belly was empty. The day wore slowly on. The sun wheeled through its zenith, descended at last into the west. Ka-Zar's mouth was hot and dry as the dust on the flags at his feet but not by one sign did he show the anguish of his body. The night would bring surcease and he had yet to test the full of his strength against the chains which bound him.

A S the long shadows fell at last across the courtyard, the blacks melted reluctantly away. Then, a moment before the sun sank below the rim of the encircling cliff, the Queen stepped silently out onto the terrace.

From long, narrowed eyes she looked down at her captive, studied him. The level shafts of the dying light glinted brightly off the jeweled ornaments that spangled her bare body, stabbed at Ka-Zar's eyes and betrayed her presence to him.

Slowly his head came up, swung toward the terrace. Coolly he surveyed the girl, a barbaric picture bathed in the warm light of the dying sun. Then his lips curled with hatred. For a long moment piercing amber eyes met glowing black ones as their gaze met and held—Tamiris, Queen of a lost civilization—Ka-Zar, Jungle King of a domain to which civilization had never come.

Tamiris' cheeks flushed and her breasts arched against the jeweled discs that covered them. A growing curiosity had brought her out to the terrace to study this strange jungle giant. Who was he, this magnificent creature who spoke with the voice of the lion? Whence came he? What did he seek in Khalli?

At the sight of his superb figure, still proudly defiant in spite of the fetters, the alien emotion that had disturbed her before came again to her heart. In a sudden confusion that she could not explain, she turned abruptly and hastily retreated from the terrace.

CHAPTER VI

Zar's Kill

T HE twilight of the tropics is brief. Purple shadows gathered at the base of the cliffs, crept silently forth and stole toward the city.

Alone at last in the courtyard, Ka-Zar watched the coming of the night. Far above him the strange, steady flame glowed brighter against the deepening sky. The hubbub of noise that had arisen steadily from the lower reaches of the city died gradually away. For the first time he could hear the distant sounds of the surrounding jungle.

The chattering of monkeys, the squawk of a sleepy bird disturbed by some prowling snake, the shrill yapping of a jackal came faintly to his ears. To Ka-Zar this was far more torture than the pangs of hunger or the torment of thirst. His soul yearned for the dark stretches of the jungle, for the wide expanse of forest and lake and star-studded heavens that were home and freedom.

His head sunk dejectedly on his breast. Now that there was no one to watch him he let his wide shoulders slump. The long strain of prolonged hunger and thirst, of the fierce rays of sun that had burned down upon him all that day, began to tell on him. A weariness of spirit as well as body descended upon him.

Then suddenly his head snapped up. From the distant jungle came a familiar cry—the rumbling bass notes of the lion's kill. The sound was distorted by the encircling cliffs, which flung it back and forth in diminishing echoes. Ka-Zar's eyes glowed. Zar—could that have been Zar?

Hardly. But if the cry was not that of his kingly brother, at least it was that of a friend. Straining his ears, he listened.

It came again—like distant thunder —challenging, triumphant. And this time Ka-Zar thrilled to every fibre of his being. For he could not be mistaken.

Too often he had exulted to that same majestic voice. Too often he had set the wilderness ringing with his own answering call. He knew that it was none other than Zar the mighty who now made the night tremble.

Ka-Zar's body stiffened to the full of his imposing height. His head tilted back, his lips opened. The first rumbling notes of the cry started in his throat—then died still-born. His jaws snapped shut.

Often during that long and terrible day he had thought of Zar and Nono and wondered at their fate. He knew now that Zar was free, that somehow he had eluded the cave-dwellers and had reached the expanse of jungle in the sunken valley. But to answer his call would have been a fatal mistake.

To the inhabitants of Khalli, the roar of a lion in the wilderness would have no significance. But let that same cry ring from the heart of the city in the darkness of the night—and instantly the courtyard would be swarming with alarmed men. If he responded to the cry—and Ka-Zar knew that his loyal brother would—Zar would only fall into a trap.

So with the consolation that at least the lion had escaped his fate, Ka-Zar let his head droop once more upon his breast. Zar could do nothing for him anyway. Despite all the strength of his massive tawny body he could not free the jungle giant of his chains.

The chains. . . .

Seizing the glittering links in his hands, Ka-Zar pulled at the hateful fetters. His powerful biceps bulged; his forearms stood out in hard knots of muscle; his broad back rippled. Beads of sweat popped out on his forehead. His brain swam giddily. In a sudden outburst of fury and desperation he gathered the last ounce of power in his flagging body, tugged and heaved.

But all his efforts availed him nought. With a bitter sigh of resignation he let the clinking chain drop from his hands. Weariness overcame him at last. His eyes dulled and his lids drooped over them. His tortured, aching body relaxed, crumpled slowly, joint by joint. He sank to the flags, crumpled at the base of the monolith. There was no need to fight against the merciful sleep that came to bathe him in oblivion.

It was a light touch that roused Ka-Zar to instant wakefulness. The stillness was absolute. The moon had risen over the Congo, but her face was wreathed in tattered wisps of cloud and only a dim, half-light pervaded the courtyard of the palace. Ka-Zar was aware, at first, only of tiny fingers on his bare arm as his eyes accustomed themselves to the darkness.

A moment later he made out his nocturnal visitor. Nono the monkey bent over him. Ka-Zar's throat was aflame with thirst. He could not even voice his gladness. Then Nono's beady-eyed face came closer; the mouth of the monkey came to meet his own.

PRECIOUS drops of water moistened Ka-Zar's dry lips. He opened them greedily and a thin stream of the fluid entered his mouth and trickled down his throat. It was tepid, but to Ka-Zar it was the elixir of life itself. Hungrily his parched body absorbed it and those few priceless drops revived him.

He struggled up to a sitting position as Nono dragged forward a chunk of raw, fresh-killed meat. Ka-Zar fell upon it and devoured it in ravenous gulps. With each mouthful new strength flowed into his weary body and the languor that had descended upon him evaporated.

"My brother's kill?" he asked the squatting monkey as he feasted.

Nono kept glancing fearfully about him. "Zar's kill," he squeaked. "Zar sent me."

Already the mouthful of water and the taste of raw meat had routed the blank despair from Ka-Zar's heart. The knowledge that he still had his two faithful allies to help him gave him new courage, new hope. The old instinct to survive, to cling to life, was strong within him.

"The silly, long-tailed one has proved a true friend to Ka-Zar," he whispered to the monkey. "If he would do more —let him bring more of the water. Nono is agile, Nono is swift. Nono can move like a silent shadow. Go—steal one of the gourds which the Oman use to carry water. Bring Ka-Zar to drink."

With a single clucking sound to show that he understood, the little creature scampered like a huge spider across the courtyard. For a brief instant his slender form was outlined against the full glow of the moon, then he vanished.

He reappeared a short time later, hugging a clay vessel in his skinny arms. Ka-Zar took it from him, drank first sparingly and then with long draughts of the cool liquid.

When the last drop had been drained, he handed the pot back to the monkey. "Take the gourd—keep it," he ordered. "Bring water to Ka-Zar when it is needed. And tell my brother the mighty Zar to lie low in the jungle."

He stood erect, a sculptured figure with one bronze arm raised in farewell, as the monkey left him.

CHAPTER VII

JUNGLE MIRACLE

IN the palace, another had found no restful sleep that night. Queen Tamiris, after tossing fitfully on her resplendent couch, had risen at last to pace the length of her magnificent chamber. Lanterns of pierced bronze that glittered with multi-colored lights, hung pendent from the high ceiling. Columns of glittering bits of mirror, cunningly set into clay, shimmered against the walls. The fragrance of burning sandalwood rose in a cloud from a huge urn and permeated the room. Luxurious rugs covered the floor and silken cushions covered the royal couch and several divans. But tonight all this evidence of queenly splendor gave Tamiris no comfort.

A frown made a deep V between her straight, dark brows. Before her eyes was always the vision of the strange jungle giant, chained to the monolith. With growing fury she thought how this man, who had come unbidden and unwanted to Khalli, had upset her carefully laid plans.

Her first test—her rights as supreme ruler against the insidious dictatorship of Zut—had come and she had failed. It was all the fault of this naked jungle savage. He had dared to insult her and in her fury, she had blindly acceded to the wishes of the usurping Zut.

Her tiny feet in their gilded sandals made no sound on the deep-piled rugs as she paced back and forth across the room.

In vain she tried to forget her fatal blunder, tried to formulate some new plan to break Zut's power and quell the incipient rebellion of the degenerate slaves. Always her mind came back to the naked bronze savage she had doomed to a lingering death.

With clenched fists she confronted the tawny-eyed vision before her. "The fault is your own that you must die thus," she whispered passionately. "Tamiris is not needlessly cruel. But in this game of empire you have made yourself a pawn. You have interfered with the plans of a Ptolemy—and so you must die."

Angry with herself, she tried to turn that anger into a mounting hate for this man whose image had come to disturb her. Wildly she prayed that he had already succumbed, so that she need no longer think of him.

And so it was that the first slanting sunbeams of the new day found her, garbed in sheer black draperies and bedecked with gold and silver, making her way toward the courtyard. Her heart was beating strangely faster in her breast as she stepped out onto the terrace.

Already a group of blacks had come to gloat upon the fate of their captive. But Tamiris found these slaves in a hushed, whispering group, gazing openmouthed at the monolith.

Her gaze shifted to one corner of her long, slitted eyes, expecting to see the jungle giant in a limp huddle at its base. She stifled the gasp that came to her lips. For there, standing more arrogantly than ever, was Ka-Zar.

There was no visible sign of the ordeal to which he had been subjected. His level eyes were just as inscrutable, his lips just as scornful, his head just as high as it had been when he had first been chained to the shaft.

One of the blacks, braver than his fellows, went closer and essayed feebly to repeat the taunts and gibes with which they had showered him the day before. But the others turned to face the Queen and in their dull, ashy faces she could read baffled wonder, baffled rage and a growing uneasiness towards this stranger.

Had they dared to approach her, they would have sought an answer to this miracle. And biting her scarlet underlip, Tamiris realized that she would have been unable to answer their question.

Other blacks came—came to stare and wonder. Swiftly Tamiris turned and in a growing perplexity that she did not dare to show, vanished once more into the palace.

ANOTHER day passed. And another. And another. And still the strange bronze giant faced each flaming sunrise in the full of his glorious strength.

All Khalli buzzed with a growing excitement. The uneasiness of the superstitious blacks who dwelled in the catacombs mounted. Each night they wended their way to the dim temple in the bowels of the earth and weird rites were performed at the feet of their ugly god. Seti, the crafty High Priest of Pthos, seized his opportunity. He pointed out that the mysterious captive was in the outer city, where Isis was the ruling deity. It was a sign that the power of Isis and of Ra, the sun-god, was weakening. And a sign also that the long dominance of the Ptolemies was diminishing in the frail hands of a woman.

These rumors spread and came at last to the tiered city. They came to the keen ears of Zut and the Machiavellian brain of that ageless schemer mulled them carefully over.

Were the Queen's prestige alone damaged by this strange happening in Khalli, Zut would have bided his time and allowed events to take their course. But he, too, lived in Khalli and in this instance, his own power was questioned. Better than Tamiris he realized that once the blacks threw off their serfdom and ran amuck, it would take an iron hand to control them. Unless he also was to be swept into oblivion by the threatening torrent, he must act.

He found Tamiris in her own apartments, sitting upon a divan with her determined chin resting in her palm. Her cheeks were flushed darkly and her ivory brow was wrinkled in a frown. She had just come from a brief visit to the courtyard.

Zut made a deep obeisance. "Daughter of the Sun," he said gravely, "I come as a friend and as a loyal counsellor. As the trusted servant of your father before you, I dare to speak the truth; as one whose years are so many more than your own, I dare to advise you."

Tamiris moved her head in a barely perceptible nod. "Speak, then," she said coldly.

Zut bowed again. "This naked, animal man fails to die. By some miracle he survives without food or water. Even Zut in his wisdom is puzzled and the blacks who dwell in the caves are greatly affected. It is as though this jungle-man defies the will of the Queen in refusing to die when she has condemned him."

Tamiris leaped to her feet, stiffened her slight body and clenched her hands at her sides. Her eyes flashed. "For once, Zut speaks the truth. Tamiris will have no more of such brazen defiance. Come. I shall speak the word and the blacks will fall upon him with their spears and swords. We shall see whether he is invulnerable to the bite of pointed steel."

The pale moonstone on Zut's finger glinted as he raised a claw-like hand. "Well-spoken, Favored of the Goddess. But for days the people have been in a state of growing tension. Such a hasty execution would not still the emotions that have been aroused. Such a swift death would be too merciful for one who has dared to bring the wrath of the Queen upon his head. No. I have a better plan."

He leaned forward and there was a glint in his close-set eyes as he spoke rapidly and earnestly to the listening girl.

A slow tide of color crept up from her heaving breast and mounted up the ivory column of her throat. Twin fringes of jet lashes dropped over her eyes to veil their depths. Then as Zut finished, she answered huskily: "It shall be as you say. Choose a hundred picked men, equip them with what they ask and send them into the forest. And let there be no delay."

With an humble attitude that did not betray his elation at this second triumph, Zut bowed and hurried off to carry out her orders.

When he had gone, Tamiris walked unsteadily over to the nearest window and stared, unseeing, out over the expanse of her isolated, buried kingdom.

CHAPTER VIII

Blood Brothers

AT first Ka-Zar exulted over the consternation of his captors. His own simple animal soul had never known the hold of superstition. Had he understood their strange language, he would have been as baffled as they. Miracles, gods and goddesses had no meaning for him.

Often he marveled at their stupidity in not setting a guard over him in the night time, wondered why they did not suspect that somehow he was obtaining food and drink. True, the courtyard was surrounded on three sides by a high wall and on the fourth, by the towering facade of the palace. Occasionally men did make surreptitious visits to his open prison during the night. But Nono was swift and noiseless and cunning and he left no tell-tale tracks on the bare flags.

But though Ka-Zar did not die, the hateful fetters were still about his neck. With each passing day he became more conscious of the symbol of his bondage. They weighed more heavily on his spirit than on his body. Despite the instinctive urge to survive, he could not restrain a vague wish that even death should come to end his monotonous and hateful captivity.

Each night he had heard the familiar roar of his tawny brother, trembling faintly across the still air. Each night the sound had whipped his flagging spirits, given him new courage to face the coming of another dawn. Then one night, as he waited with a faint smile on his lips for the cry of his brother, he heard a new note in the lion's voice.

Ka-Zar's heart froze to an icy lump within him as the lion's roar rang out again and again from the distant jungle. This was not the triumphant pronouncement of another kill. There was a note of fury, of desperation, in the sound. Tense, drawn, his face set in lines of anguish, Ka-Zar stood rigid at the base of the monolith and listened. With a sinking feeling at the pit of his stomach he knew that now the sounds coming from Zar's mighty throat were compounded of baffled rage and pain. They were echoed by a concerted howl, fiendish shrieks of triumph from the lips of many Omen.

A short time later, Nono scampered over the wall. In the stress of his excitement he had brought neither meat nor water. Ka-Zar seized him as he approached.

"Zar?" he asked in a guttural growl. "What has happened to Zar?"

His teeth chattering with fright, Nono confirmed his worst fears. Omen—many Omen—had crept quietly into the forest. The mighty Zar had been captured by a trick and now he lashed helplessly in a great cage.

Ka-Zar took the blow in stoic silence. Already the first wan tinge of dawn was lightening the east. Enveloped by a poignant grief such as he had never known, he bowed his head as Nono disappeared from the courtyard.

Sunk in silent apathy, Ka-Zar had not yet moved when the first blacks came as usual to look upon him. Dully he raised his head and from lack-lustre eyes he surveyed them.

Now their manner towards him was radically changed. Triumph was in their harsh voices. An unholy anticipation gleamed in their sunken eyes. They forgot their recent fears and gathered in a milling throng to torment him.

That some new plan for deviltry was afoot, Ka-Zar could readily see. He longed to understand the outlandish chatter of these jackals so that he might learn the fate of his brother. He was indifferent to his own. After all, though he had forsworn them, he was actually one of the despised two-legged species. He had some understanding of the dark impulses that motivated them, that had led them to fetter him with chains. But the animal brain of Zar was yet simpler than his own. Ka-Zar's heart bled for the sufferings of the king of the jungle, finding himself penned up by hateful bars.

Occasionally, above the chatter of these yapping jackals, he heard the angry voice of Zar, each time nearer to the city. And as the sun climbed higher in the heavens more people than ever before appeared to congregate in the courtyard.

This time, apprehension came to Ka-Zar's troubled brain. It was soon evident that some momentous event was due to happen. Zut appeared on a balcony high above the terrace, a striking figure despite the simplicity of his garb. The white dwellers of Khalli, dressed in brilliant, outlandish costume, joined the throng. Like Zut, they were tall, swarthy of skin and hawk-eyed, hooknosed and bearded.

A MAN Ka-Zar had never seen before, but obviously a personage of importance, appeared beside Zut on the balcony. Seti, the High Priest of Pthos, was a glittering but repellent figure. He was fat to the point of obscenity. His features were all but invisible in his doughy, putty-colored face. His priestly vestments swathed an enormous paunch and he waddled as he walked. Soon he and Zut had their heads together in low but earnest conclave.

The noise and confusion mounted. Still Ka-Zar neither moved nor spoke. Only his watchful eyes observed them all and his busy brain tried to guess what was to come.

A sudden hush fell over the multitude. All eyes in the courtyard turned upward toward the balcony. There was a concerted intake of breath and then as one man they prostrated themselves face downward upon the flags.

Ka-Zar's eyes flicked upward. On the balcony, flanked by the deferential figures of Zut and Seti, ringed about by female attendants and tall Egyptian soldiers, stood Tamiris. A huge peacock feather fan shaded her from the brilliant rays of the sun. An elaborate headdress of gems and feathers covered her sleek hair and a fabric woven of shimmering metal threads was wrapped about her slender hips. Her face was pale and her eyes were darkly-burning coals in a wan mask.

Just for one fleeting moment did her glance rest on the captive. A swift intuition told Ka-Zar that it was in the last futile hope that he showed signs of weakness. But he did not know why she wished this. And so with the ghost of a smile he mocked her and was pleased to see that her bosom rose and fell as she tore her eyes away. Instead, she looked out over the west wall.

What she saw there made her eyes widen. She leaned forward with sinuous grace, grasped the edge of the balcony. Ka-Zar was reminded of N'Jagi the black leopard. There was the same savage beauty, the same lithe grace, the same feline cruelty in every line of them both. Both aroused the same instinctive antagonism in his heart.

Tamiris raised her hand and a brilliant sunlight was reflected from a score of tinkling bracelets that encircled her bare arm. Her husky tones floated out over the prone multitude in unmistakeable command.

The gathering came hastily to its feet. Like a receding tide blacks and Egyptians swept back from the monolith, helped one another scale the walls and perched safely atop them. Every balcony of the palace was crowded, other spectators peered down from the roof and from the topmost tiers of the city.

Alone in the deserted courtyard, Ka-Zar knew that the ordeal had come. His anxious eyes sought the faces of the people who had come to witness. All were looking out beyond the west wall and he alone could not see what waited there.

Then startlingly near, like a throbbing reverberation of a mighty thunder, came the roar of Zar the lion. The spectators gasped, cried out, then cheered.

At the sound of his brother's voice, Ka-Zar jerked as though he had been struck. It was Zar—Zar in his cage—who was on the other side of that high blank wall. The knowledge that he was so near his friend brought a sudden surge of relief.

And then that relief died in Ka-Zar's heart. A ghastly thought came to his brain. These crafty Omen — these wicked creatures with their twisted souls and twisted brains—had found the supreme torture for their captive. By some cunning trick they had captured Zar and now they intended to slay his blood brother before his own horrified eyes!

For the first time Ka-Zar's stoic calm was completely shattered. In a frenzy born of desperation, his brain filled only with the dire need of his friend, he went berserk. As though the chain that bound him was a living thing he seized it, grappled with it, tore at it. He clawed at the bronze collar around his throat. But the glittering links held and mocked him with their slender strength.

THE assembled multitude saw his sudden outburst and misinterpreting it, shrieked with delight. Ka-Zar stared up at the Queen, his lips pulled back from his teeth in a snarl, his tawny eyes glinting through a shock of touseled hair, his handsome features distorted into a scowl of hate. He longed to climb up onto the balcony and spring upon her slender figure. He breathed a silent prayer that he would live long enough to get his chance and vowed that when he did, his huge hands would encircle that ivory column of throat and squeeze the breath of life from it.

But again all eyes had shifted away from his figure. He followed their direction and saw a small section of the west wall—a cunningly-concealed door whose existence he had not suspected—open slowly inward.

Again there was a clamor of the multitude and to a blood-curdling chorus of howls and shrieks, echoed by another rumbling roar, an enormous tawny shape bounded through the portal.

Zar, roused to a frenzy by the jabs of many spearheads, charged into the courtyard. A red film of hate dimmed his eyes. A smouldering fury burned in his breast. Like a yellow hurricane of death he sprang at the only creature he saw before him. His great fangs were bared and his talon-like claws were arched to rip the hated Om to ribbons.

The mad chorus of the onlookers rose to a shrill pitch. Tamiris leaned forward again, gripping the rail of the balcony until her knuckles stood out white beneath the skin. All the color had gone from her face. A thousand emotions in turn crawled over her features and her dark eyes were haunted.

Oblivious to the din, Ka-Zar stared at the tawny fury that catapulted toward him. A strange half-whine, half-growl tore from his lips. It was the same sound, though no other knew it, that Zar's cubs would make when Sha their mother cuffed them too roughly.

The massive body of Zar jerked in mid-air. He landed on stiffened forelegs, slid to a sudden halt that brought him up short at the feet of the man chained to the monolith.

The shrieks of the crowd rose to fever-pitch. Then they were stilled as though a sudden stroke had paralyzed every throat. This lion was the most enormous beast they had ever seen. They were prepared for the sight of a terrible, bloody slaughter. But they were not prepared to see the bronze giant stoop to the limit of his chain, throw his arms about the neck of the lion and bury his face in the beast's shaggy mane!

For the space of long seconds no one stirred; no one spoke. It was as though the walls and the balconies and the ramparts of Khalli were lined with images of stone. And in that moment Ka-Zar knew at last the fate that the Queen had planned for him. She did not know he he was the king of the jungle, lord of the jungle beasts.

For a last precious second he clung to his mighty brother. Then he rose, turned to face the balcony where Tamiris, Zut, Seti and the rest still stood petrified with astonishment, and flung back his head and laughed.

Zar rose from his crouch, strode to Ka-Zar's side and turned to face the silent audience. A regal pair — magnificent specimen of man and beast— they confronted their enemies with kingly dignity.

The silence was shattered as abruptly as it had fallen. With a piercing shriek a black flung his arms to the unseeing heavens, wailed in terror and then buried his face in his hands. The spell once shattered, the others broke out in a confused clamor. Some, trying to flee, fought in blind panic against the packed throng that hemmed them in. From the balcony Tamiris shouted an order, but her voice was drowned by the tumult and none heard.

Ka-Zar was quick to sense the brief advantage. He leaned over and growled something low to Zar. For a moment the lion hesitated. Then the caution, that along with his might had made him ruler of the wilderness, made him see the wisdom of Ka-Zar's command.

Without warning he loosed another earth-shaking bellow. His captors had underestimated his prowess. Two tremendous leaps took him to the nearest wall, he gathered his great haunches and another bound catapulted him to the top. Screaming men spilled in every direction. One stroke of Zar's death-dealing paw sent another hurtling far out through the air, his last mortal cry quivering from his lips. Then before the startled assemblage could recover either their courage or their wits, the great lion was gone.

CHAPTER IX

TEST OF THE GODS

UP on the royal balcony the Queen, the High Priest and Zut were as dumfounded as the ignorant slaves below. Zut, by far the keenest of the three, was the first to realize the full possibilities of the situation. Whether he had indeed witnessed another miracle, or whether the strange jungle man had worked some mysterious black art on the charging lion, he was not sure.

But he was the first to note the change in the attitude of the Egyptians and the blacks below.

The cave dwellers in particular had forgotten that a short few moments before, they had cried for the blood of the victim. Now as they recovered from their first shock, they gazed upon him with open-mouthed awe. There was both respect and fear in their faces.

Zut's cunning brain interpreted his knowledge swiftly. The blacks had seen a miracle—this creature, to them, was a god! At least, it would need but a single voicing of that thought to bring them all to their knees. Zut suddenly changed his mind about the fate of this prisoner. In his supreme ego and ambition he decided that he could make use of such a god.

Tamiris' reaction was entirely different. As Zut had said, this lion-man's refusal to die was a personal affront. And each day that he continued to live, increased her agitation about him. She grew furious at him—mainly because she sensed that she—a daughter of the Ptolemies—was weakening.

Seti saw only that she was quivering with rage. He waddled forward, made an awkward bow.

"Daughter of Isis," he pleaded, "this man desecrated the Temple of Pthos by his unbelieving presence. The followers of Pthos demand his death. Let Pthos himself decide his fate."

In spite of her fury, the Queen blanched. "Seti means . . . ?"

The High Priest bobbed his bald head. "Yes, Daughter of the Pharoahs. Let him drain the Cup of Pthos. If the god wills that he be spared, he will live. If he has angered the god, he will surely die."

Tamiris' face grew sombre. The Cup of Pthos was a draught of the bitter waters of a poisoned spring, that bubbled in a cavern far under the cliffs. Three times in her life she had seen suspected traitors drain the chalice. In each instance the ordeal had proven them guilty, for each man had died writhing in excrutiating agony. She hesitated.

Zut stepped forward, bowed. "Would it be wise, O Queen?" he demurred. "Look. See your subjects down below —see . . .."

For once in his life, Zut had made a bad tactical error. Tamiris whirled on him, her eyes flashing fire. "So! Zut dares to dictate to his sovereign? Skulking schemer! Base usurper of the right of Kings! In a woman you have met your master! I hear you and I defy you!"

All the carefully thought out words with which she had planned to deliver her challenge were forgotten in her passion. In an uncontrolled outburst she cursed Zut with all the unspeakable curses of the ancient gods. Then in a last paroxysm of rage her hand lashed out quick as a snake and her open palm struck the side of Zut's gaunt cheek. It fell away, leaving the livid imprint of five fingers that all could see. And leaving, what they could not see—a wound in his warped soul that would never heal.

Whirling to face Seti, Tamiris commanded: "Send one of your men, swiftly, for the Cup."

Then conscious that she had thrown down the fateful gauntlet, she turned and grasped the railing of the balcony once more.

Seti called down to one of the awe-struck slaves. Zut stepped back a pace. The imprint of the Queen's hand paled slowly on his cheeks as he combed his straggly beard with one hand, twirled the moonstone ring on his finger with the other. But there was a glint in his close-set eyes that no one had ever seen before and the other people on the balcony shrank imperceptibly away from him.

STILL standing alone in the court-yard, Ka-Zar, too, had noticed the change that had fallen over the multitude. Though he was still in chains, no longer were gibes and insults hurled at him. Instead he noted with secret amusement the awe and respect in the faces now turned toward him. It appeared, though he did not experience as vast a relief as an ordinary man would have known, that he was to be spared further torment.

And so it was that when at last a black entered the courtyard, bearing a small chalice, that he suspected no treachery. The slave's respectful attitude, was in fact, genuine. As he came up to the monolith and proffered the cup with a reverent bow, Ka-Zar remembered that in the excitement of Zar's capture the night before, Nono had forgotten to bring him water. He was t h i r s t y and unsuspecting, he reached eagerly for the chalice.

Had he glanced up at the royal balcony as he touched his lips to the brimming cup, had he seen the deep anguish in the eyes of the Queen, he would have dashed it from him. But instead he drank.

The water was bitter, unpleasant to the taste. But thirstily he drained the vessel to the last drop.

Even as the slave retreated with the empty chalice, he felt the first pangs. Then for the first time he realized his mistake. A single, sweeping glance at the tense faces above him confirmed his suspicions.

A slow fire burned at his vitals. The pain of it mounted swiftly to an agony of torment. Ka-Zar was sure, then, that his last hour had come. He only prayed that the torment would end swiftly, before even his iron will would break and he would betray his suffering to the human fiends who watched him.

Stabbing darts of flame shot through his body. The insidious poison spread swiftly, numbing his limbs. He knew that he was powerless to move, even if he tried. He bit his tongue to keep from crying out as liquid fire coursed through his veins.

But such was his iron self-control that the watchers could see no visible evidence that the poison was taking effect. Only Zut was keen-eyed enough to discern the beads of sweat that bedewed the suffering giant's forehead and guess the truth.

Without seeming to move fast he sidled off the balcony.

"Another drink—of mere water—to hasten the work of the poison," he muttered and disappeared before the startled Queen might stop him.

A moment later he reappeared on the terrace and stepped down into the courtyard. In response to his command a slave hurried off, came back bearing a clay pot of water. Zut took it from him and walked up to the agonized Ka-Zar.

The film that had descended over the latter's eyes cleared just long enough for him to recognize Zut and to see what happened as the Queen's counsellor proffered him the drink. For a moment Ka-Zar believed that his brain was already poisoned and that it was all part of a ghastly nightmare when Zut performed a swift bit of legerdemain over the cup.

But the rays of the sun glinted on the huge moonstone and Ka-Zar could plainly see Zut's claw-like fingers loosen the stone with a single twist; could plainly see the stone hinge back and a fine white powder sift into the clay pot.

More poison? There was no need for that. He was already doomed. But even if by chance it were, it would perhaps end his agony more swiftly. When Zut raised the vessel to his lips, he drank avidly.

Zut waited until he had drained all the potion. Then as though through awkwardness he let the pot slip through his fingers and shatter into shards on the flags. Then stepping back he watched Ka-Zar through half-closed eyes.

FOR a moment of crucial agony Ka-Zar dug his nails deep into the palms of his hands and prayed that his next breath would be his last. Then gradually, to his growing wonder, the fires of torture began to die down. The leaden feeling left his limbs. His body was still racked with pain but it was definitely lessening.

Zut saw the first tinge of healthy color come back to the stricken giant's face. He saw the man's tense limbs gradually relax. He saw the tawny eyes clear, saw them turn to him in dumb gratitude.

He fingered the moonstone ring. In all Khalli, only he possessed the secret of the white powder, which was an antidote for the lethal waters of the poison spring. Against the day when he himself might have to undergo the ordeal, the ring in which the powder was cunningly concealed had never left his finger. Now, smarting under the outrage the Queen had committed against him, he had found ready use for it.

Zut could not read the lion-man's thoughts, but that did not matter, for what ensued was sufficient for his own purpose.

As the pain left him and his brain cleared, Ka-Zar's first thought was that Zar was free and he himself had still survived. The warm surge of life swept through his veins, exhilarated him. He turned his face toward the sun that he had thought he would never see again, raised his fists to his brawny chest and with a thunderous bellow, sent the roar of the lion echoing over the heads of the silent multitude.

As though this were a signal, blacks and Egyptians alike set up a mournful wail. And Zut seized the chance for which he had been waiting.

Stepping forward, he raised both arms dramatically to the watching throng.

"Men of Khalli!" he cried. "The god has spoken! Henceforth whosoever harms this man's sacred person—let him beware—for he shall incur the wrath of Pthos!"

Shouting, yelling, pushing, his listeners poured over the walls and jammed the courtyard. They dropped on their knees before Ka-Zar, touched their foreheads humbly to the flags to beg his forgiveness.

Zut turned his eyes toward the royal balcony. "Even the Pharoahs," he cried out, "bow before the will of the gods. Daughter of the Sphinx—give the order to liberate this man who is favored of Pthos!"

All through the ordeal Tamiris had remained clutching the rail of the balcony. Now she looked down into the sea of expectant faces upturned to her own. Again Zut dared to command her!

Dimly she sensed that somehow he had tricked her. In helpless fury she saw that the black descendants of the the slaves were with him to a man. It was their god who had spoken. If she dared to refuse—the submerged fires of rebellion would break out into instant flame. A single glance showed her that the blacks outnumbered the residents of Khalli in hopeless measure. The cave-dwellers would fall upon them and wipe out her people in a swift and terrible massacre. Ankhamen, the stalwart leader of her army, and her soldiers surrounded the courtyard. But they were too few—too few. . . .

Somehow she found her voice. Somehow she managed to speak the command.

Instantly the horde leaped to their feet and surrounded Ka-Zar. The key to his bonds was produced amid cheers. Willing hands loosed the chain from the ring in the monolith, then jerked the bronze collar from his throat. Seti lumbered across the balcony, entered the palace and a moment later joined the crowd in the courtyard.

It was only Tamiris' hold on the balcony that kept her steady on her feet. Her pride had suffered many blows, she had made a powerful enemy in Zut, her high-handed ambitions were dangerously threatened. Yet though her world trembled beneath her feet, she watched Ka-Zar being freed with relief instead of displeasure.

Her face, however, was inscrutable. And when the collar dropped from his neck and he glanced up at her, he could not guess that in her heart of hearts she exulted with him. Without a word, without a gesture, she watched him as flanked by Zut and Seti and with a mob of howling, grinning blacks at his heels, he was escorted in triumph from the palace.

CHAPTER X

Sacrifice to Pthos

WITH Zut as his mentor, Ka-Zar began a new life in Khalli. The freedom of the tiered city, of the jungle, of the caverns, was his. He roamed where he willed and everywhere he was greeted with the respect which was now his due.

Under Zut's tutelage he made rapid progress learning the language of this lost people. He owed a debt to this ageless, enigmatic man who had saved his life. Ka-Zar had his own code of honor —a strange compound of the teachings of his dead father and the jungle code of the beasts. Some day he would repay that debt.

The first thing that he did, as soon as he could escape the homage of the worshiping blacks, was to set out alone toward the forest that lay between the city and the opening in the cliffs that led to the underground lake and the caverns. His call of the lion immediately brought an answer from Zar and soon his brother and the little monkey joined him on the shady jungle floor.

In the limited vocabulary of growls and grunts that was the language of the beasts, he told them of his new freedom. It was possible that Zar might once more take his place by his brother's side, but the wise old lion preferred the familiar haunts of the wilderness. It was Nono, on his favorite perch atop the bronze giant's shoulder, who accompanied Ka-Zar back to the city.

That was the first of many surreptitious visits during which the trio decided that they would undertake the seemingly hopeless task of finding a way out of this sunken valley. In the heart of each was a longing for their distant jungle home, that grew with each passing day until it became a driving obsession.

The people of Khalli marveled when Ka-Zar appeared with the little monkey clinging to him, marveled still more when it was seen that man and beast spoke to one another. The only one who really understood was Zut. To his new-found friend, in his newly-acquired tongue, Ka-Zar explained his life in the wilderness, his dominance over the beasts and the manner in which he had arrived in Khalli. And that was why Zut alone knew that this bronze giant was but a man, however a strange one. He knew why the massive lion had failed to slay him and he shrewdly guessed that this little monkey was the reason that Ka-Zar had not died of hunger and of thirst in the courtyard. And so, though he was careful to pay due homage to his protege before the eyes of others, he was merely friendly when they were alone.

Ka-Zar avoided the palace. On several occasions he glimpsed the Queen, once when she was on her way to the Temple of Isis, once when she appeared at a festival. But each time he kept well out of sight, grateful that he no longer had to suffer her hateful presence.

His mind was filled day and night with the desire to escape. Having an instinctive dislike for the underground catacombs and the creatures of darkness who dwelled in them, he began his explorations in the open bowl of the sunken valley. Sometimes Zar accompanied them, sometimes he and Nono were alone. The high wall of cliffs was many miles in circumference. Starting first from a point north of the city, Ka-Zar prowled about their base. Time and again he found openings in the rock, entered only to find that they were shallow caves that had no other outlet. Time and again he found a precipitate path leading up the face of the walls, scaled it at perilous risk only to reach a point beyond which neither man nor beast could ascend higher.

Every home, every cave in Khalli was open to him. He would return weary in body and limb, sleep in mansion or in jungle, and with the next sunrise be off again on his ceaseless quest.

And so it was that he failed to notice the ever-growing tension in the isolated kingdom. Many times he found Zut and Seti with their heads together in solemn conclave, but he did not guess that they were surreptitiously stirring up the simmering brew of rebellion.

ONE evening, as he was just about to set forth for the jungle to find Zar and report another day of fruitless search, a slave came running to him, flung himself on the ground at his feet and panted a message.

"All day, O Favored of Pthos," said the black breathlessly, "Zut has sought you. He desires your presence at once in the Temple of Pthos."

With distaste, Ka-Zar remembered the dim underground chamber where he had first been made captive. It was on his tongue to refuse, then he remembered also the debt he owed to Zut. Reluctantly he made a gesture to the black to rise. "Very well. Come."

Together they made the journey down the long road that had been hewn through the heart of the jungle. Not many ventured to traverse it after nightfall. Now the black strode hurriedly along the dim forest floor, his eyes fearfully searching the shadows on either side. A faint smile flitted across Ka-Zar's lips each time the man's face turned ashen at the howl of a hyena, the scurrying of a rodent across the trail or the mysterious rustling of branches overhead.

They came at last to the break in the cliffs, turned into the tunnels lighted with flaring torches. This was the first time since his capture that Ka-Zar had returned to the place of caves and catacombs. But he had not forgotten the dank, foul air that rushed to assail his nostrils now, the vast, dark reach of the underground lake, the constant drip, drip of water.

This time, though, free and with no need for caution, he saw things that he had not noticed before. There were boats drawn up along the shores of the lake—high-prowed vessels painted in red and black and yellow, with figureheads of carven monsters. He saw bats, enormous creatures, who flitted through the tunnels on phantom wings and hung in great pendent clusters from the rocky roof. He saw wrinkled hags, incredibly ragged and dirty, steal from the catacombs, fill clay pots with water from the lake and scurry back into their holes again.

"Where are the men?" Ka-Zar asked his companion.

"They are already in the temple," answered the slave. "There is to be a ceremony."

The answer meant little to Ka-Zar. He asked no more. He found Zut waiting for him in the corridor, at the exact place where he had left Zar that first fateful night.

Zut dismissed the slave, then bowed to Ka-Zar. "Tonight there is a sacred rite in the temple," he explained. "A sacrifice is to be offered to Pthos and Seti, the High Priest, has given you the great honor of performing the task that is reserved only for his own holy hands."

Ka-Zar shook his head. "I know not what you mean. This matter of gods and ceremony and such is beyond my comprehension. I want none of it."

"It is to honor Pthos," reminded Zut gravely. "Remember, it was Pthos who spared you."

Ka-Zar did not believe that. But his own eyes had seen this man save him. With the reminder of his debt, reluctantly he agreed to accompany Zut into the temple.

They opened the heavy bronze door and stepped into the great chamber beyond. The temple was jammed with a dense throng of blacks, squatting on the floor before the towering image of their god. On the dais, at the feet of the hideous statue, stood Seti. His obese form swathed in multi-colored raiment, he stood with arms upraised and a weird chant issued from his lips.

Ka-Zar stepped a little to one side, then suddenly he stiffened as a low snarl sounded directly behind him. He whirled about and the hairs crawled at the back of his neck. Twin orbs of emerald glared balefully back at him. For a moment of stark unbelief, Ka-Zar stared at the ebony form of N'Jagi, the black leopard.

Instinctively Ka-Zar fell into a crouch and a low growl rumbled in his throat as he waited for N'Jagi to spring. Then he saw that the leopard was chained. Glittering links fastened his collar to a ring set in the wall. That explained why the blacks were able to worship here in the temple without fear of the beast.

IN hate and fear, N'Jagi laid his ears flat back against his narrow skull, curled his lips back from his sharp fangs and spat. Zut came over hurriedly, walked up to the leopard, laid a hand upon the animal's flat head, spoke low, soothing words. N'Jagi subsided, only his eyes glaring malevolently at his enemy.

"So the leopard did not die?" said Ka-Zar.

"No," answered Zut. "He was sorely wounded, unconscious. But I have nursed him back to health and he is once more guardian of the temple."

"You do not fear him, like the rest," said Ka-Zar.

Zut shook his head. "No. It was I who raised him from a cub. It is I who feed him. The leopard knows me and loves me and would lay down his life to defend me."

Again Ka-Zar had occasion to be puzzled by the ways of these Omen. N'Jagi was Zut's brother, even as he himself was the brother of Zar. If man or beast harmed either one, the other would hunt the culprit down and slay him. Yet Ka-Zar had almost killed N'Jagi and Zut, the leopard's master, held no resentment against him.

He shook his head, dismissing such a matter that he would never understand.

Leaving the leopard, Zut beckoned him to follow. Together they wended their way through the dense throng, gained the dais at last and mounted it. The High Priest ended his chant on a shrill, high note.

"Do as Seti tells you," Zut whispered to Ka-Zar, then drew back to a shadowy corner.

Slaves replenished the burning braziers and the flames mounted higher. As Seti came toward Ka-Zar, the assemblage touched their heads twice to the floor before them, then fell to a slow, rhythmic swaying.

Ill at ease, wishing that the cursed rites were over, Ka-Zar submitted to his role. He allowed Seti to drape a resplendent cloak over his naked body, allowed him to set a headdress in the form of a golden, winged lion upon his brow, allowed him to thrust a golden wand that ended in a serpent's head into his hand.

"Do as I do," hissed the High Priest in his ear.

And because of his debt to Zut, Ka-Zar obeyed.

The strange ceremony that followed was ever after a blur in Ka-Zar's mind. The air was close and oppressive with the scent of many unwashed bodies. The light was dimmed by the clouds of smoke that issued from the braziers. Sometimes the crowd was hushed as Seti harangued them; sometimes there was a hubbub as all tongues broke out into a babble. Twice a black shrieked, writhed about on the floor frothing at the mouth, and was carried out by his fellows. Once N'Jagi, aroused by the sight of his old enemy, made the vaulted chamber ring with his hideous screech.

Ka-Zar was not yet proficient enough in the language to understand it when it was sung in minor chants or spoken in a swift torrent of passionate words. But he did see that the assembled cave dwellers were working themselves up to a higher and higher pitch. Strange music added to the bedlam. From off to one side came the clash of brazen cymbals, the thin, reedy wail of a flute, the muffled beating of a drum.

Again Seti raised his arms to the leering face of the god looking down upon them. Then he turned and looked off to the left. There was a stir in that direction. A small door opened. The assembled worshippers craned their necks, then raised their voices in a concerted shout of anticipation.

Ka-Zar looked, also. He saw a slave, bound with heavy ropes, shoved forward toward the dais by the eager hands of his fellows. The man was in the grip of abject terror. His knees trembled so that he could hardly move. His eyes were wide open in blank despair. His loose lips quivered, but no sound issued from them.

ONCE on the dais, he dropped to a kneeling position as the High Priest turned once more to address the god. Ka-Zar saw the blood lust on the faces of the worshippers. When Seti had finished, he walked to the edge of the platform, received something from another slave.

Ka-Zar saw the dim light reflected on a huge, naked sword. Its curved blade, he could see even at that distance, was keen and razor-sharp. In blank amazement he watched Seti waddle toward him and before he could recover his wits, the monstrous weapon was in his own hands.

The High Priest gestured toward the kneeling man. The words he spoke were lost in the deafening clamor that rang out from the crowd.

Dumbly Ka-Zar stepped forward— one step, two, three. . . .

Then at last he realized what was expected of him. He was expected to use that sword—he was expected to slay the terrified victim. A swift vision crossed before his eyes. He could see the hapless creature already dead—see the warm blood trickling down over the steps of the dais while the bloodthirsty mob shrieked their delight.

He raised the sword. Then with all his might he flung the glittering weapon at the foot of the idol!

The shriek froze in every throat. A hush as profound as the stillness of death fell upon the temple, as all faces stared in shocked amazement. Such a thing had never happened before.

And in that utter silence Ka-Zar denounced them.

"Despised Oman!" he cried, his amber eyes blazing and his huge hands clenched. "To think that Ka-Zar—brother of Zar the mighty—king of the beasts and the jungle—would do this shameful thing! To slay in fair battle is one thing—to slay a helpless victim is another. Crawl back into your holes—rats that you are!"

Fortunately, for him, he was still not proficient enough in his new tongue to speak it with such passionate speed. His flow of words was unintelligible.

Zut, as always, was more quick-witted than the rest. He leaped forward, took his place by Ka-Zar's side and with consummate artistry, raised both arms in a dramatic gesture.

"Again the god has spoken!" he cried. "Again Pthos commands you through his new disciple! He needs no sacrifice to appease him—he smiles upon you! His intended victim shall live to worship, in humble gratitude, the mercy of Pthos!"

Seti still had not found either his wits or his tongue. Cheated of the bloody spectacle, the mass of slaves looked sullen and disappointed. But too ignorant to question the words of such a wise man as Zut, they heard and believed. There was only a subdued mutter as Zut and Ka-Zar swiftly unbound the dazed victim and he scurried off.

Ka-Zar had had enough. With a nauseous feeling at the pit of his stomach, he stalked off the dais, strode through the crowd and left the temple.

Zut followed him, caught up to him in the passage outside. Ka-Zar surveyed his friend and mentor from cold eyes.

The latter combed his straggly beard. "Such things are the custom," he explained. "For long years the slaves have made human sacrifice to Pthos."

"Such customs are evil," retorted Ka-Zar. "If the slaves do such monstrous things, they should be punished."

Zut moved his finger, rubbed the side of his beaked nose. "I am not the ruler of this kingdom," he said slowly.

Then, having cleverly implied that she was responsible for the unholy practise, leaving Ka-Zar with a vision of the youthful Queen as he had last seen her standing on the balcony, Zut moved off.

CHAPTER XI

THE CATACOMBS

ZUT did not make the mistake of again inviting Ka-Zar to join in the worship of the evil Pthos. Free once more to renew his search for a way of escape, Ka-Zar continued his round of the valley.

But he failed to find what he sought. Though he did not relish the prospect, he decided that the underground tunnels and caverns were next.

He started out one morning just as the dawn brought a faint, pinkish tinge to the East, though in the bowels of the earth he knew it made small difference whether it was night or day. The night before he had sent Nono to Zar with a message and so he went alone on his quest.

He knew what a hopeless maze of tunnels and passages opened off the banks of the underground river and lake. Once before he had blundered headlong into trouble. It was not trouble but a way of escape that he was now seeking. Sooner or later, perhaps, he would have to try every passage. But first he would go in the direction he remembered—southward towards the spot where he and Zar and Nono had first blundered into the lost kingdom.

The cavedwellers were just beginning to stir in their lairs when he skirted the shore of the lake. The flares were sputtering low in their brackets. But Ka-Zar's eyes were like those of a great cat and his pupils widened to accustom them to the dimness. He reached the place where the river emptied its swift-flowing waters into the silent lake, turned the sharp bend and followed its slippery bank.

Again the bats wheeled on ghostly wings about his head. In the dying light of the last flare he saw great, bloated spiders crawling on the walls of the passage. The darkness deepened as he went on. Before him, reptiles he could not see slithered off the mud bank and splashed into the stream.

With sure instinct he turned at last into the tunnel through which he and his friends had first come. But as he progressed deeper, he began to wonder why the darkness did not lighten. The landslide that had brought him tumbling downward had left a gaping hole in the earth above. The daylight it admitted should have filtered to the spot where he now stood.

He found the answer fifty yards farther on. The way before him was blocked—blocked by a solid mass of earth and rock.

Ka-Zar scowled in the darkness. He remembered that the week before, a violent tropical storm had wreaked its fury upon Khalli. Perhaps the torrential rain that fell then had battered down more of the earth above, packed it in a mounting heap that blocked off the tunnel.

Morosely he turned back and returned to the river. Standing again on its bank, he hesitated for a moment. Then abruptly he turned and went further along its muddy shore. He had not gone far when he discovered another tunnel opening in the rocks. With the same dim hope that had sustained him in his quest, he turned into it.

This time, he had not gone far when he pulled up short in his tracks. A low, ominous rumbling came to his ears. It grew louder with alarming rapidity. The very earth trembled beneath his feet.

For an instant Ka-Zar was paralyzed. For an instant numb horror froze his heart. Then the spell was broken and turning, he fled blindly back through the passage.

He had not acted a moment too soon. With a reverberating roar that thundered in his ears, an avalanche of earth and stones poured after him. A shower of mud, a spatter of pebbles sprayed upon his retreating back. With a last burst of speed that threatened to burst his lungs, he reached the opening of the tunnel, sprinted a few more yards up the river bank.

Panting, he mopped the perspiration from his brow as the landslide rushed through the tunnel, came to a slithering halt upon the bank and sent a last shower of debris splashing into the water.

Once before he had been buried alive by such a treacherous torrent. Now again he had barely escaped being entombed. This was a dangerous vicinity, here in the bowels of the earth. Apparently these landslides were frequent and they came without warning.

SHAKEN by the narrowness of his escape, and yet reluctant to give up the search that by now had become a symbol of life itself to him, he did not re-trace his way at once toward Khalli. The last rumbles of the falling earth died away, leaving the silence broken only by the monotonous drip of water and the murmuring rush of the stream.

The river. Ka-Zar's brows knitted. Why had he not thought of it before? It came from somewhere—it had some source. Did it merely bubble out of the rocks from some hidden spring? He determined to find out.

Despite his better judgment, a growing hope mounted in his breast as he set off along the bank. And therefore when he had penetrated as far as he could go, he knew the keenest disappointment. He had come to a place where the stream boiled out of a hole in the rocks barely big enough to permit its passage. Whether that hole led to its very source —a spring—or whether it was but another tunnel that made a natural length of pipe, with the river widening once more beyond it, he could not guess. But no living creature could attempt to go through that aperture, through those seething waters, and live.

Bitterly Ka-Zar turned and wearily he headed back in the direction from whence he had come.

Late that same afternoon, the Queen Tamiris was on one of her frequent pilgrimages to the Temple of Isis. Surrounded by all the pomp and glitter of her court, she reclined on the soft cushions of her palanquin as slaves carried it down through the city.

Contrary to the impression she had so unfortunately made on Ka-Zar, Tamiris was honorable and just. She had a stern sense of duty and toward that duty, she would willingly sacrifice any life in Khalli if need be. But needless cruelty, the taking of life without any justification whatsoever, she could not tolerate.

At the head of her procession were several black slaves whose duty it was to clear the way. People drew respectfully back to either side of the road to make obeisance as their sovereign passed.

A mangy, homeless cur, intent only upon a morsel of refuse on the opposite side, scurried across the roadway. Though he was well in advance of the slow-moving cavalcade, one of the foremost slaves shouted angrily, stooped and picked up a great rock. He hurled it at the cowering dog with deadly accuracy.

There was a sickening thud, a single yelp of terror. Then with piteous whines the dying beast dragged itself a few more yards, collapsed, kicked once convulsively and then lay still.

Tamiris had viewed the whole incident. It had transpired too swiftly for her to intervene and spare the life of the brute. Now in a sudden flare of outraged passion, she leaped from her litter. Snatching the jeweled girdle from her hips she strode angrily toward the slave.

Ka-Zar, turning a corner, was just in time to see her confront the black—a barbaric picture of slim legs disclosed by whipping draperies, of raven hair tossed by the wind and eyes like great pools of jet.

He saw the culprit fling himself face downward in the dust, saw the Queen's right arm flash up. The glittering girdle described a short arc through the air, then descended with all her might across the back of the slave. The sharp-cut gems bit deep into the bare flesh, leaving a long welt that turned slowly scarlet. Once more the lash rose and fell and a second raw stripe criss-crossed the first.

Then with a gesture of revulsion Tamiris flung the glittering girdle into the dust, turned on her heel and returned to her palanquin.

At the first stroke of the lash Ka-Zar knew a momentary impulse to leap out and interfere. Then he downed it. Queen or slave—these Oman were nothing to him. Let them torture or slay each other, if it pleased them to do so he did not care.

He had, so he thought, witnessed just one more display of cruelty on the part of this bloodthirsty female. Soundlessly he stepped back into a nearby doorway and waited, silent and unseen, while the procession went past.

When it had gone he emerged and slowly headed for the palace in search of Zut.

CHAPTER XII

INTRIGUE

THE attendants and soldiers at the gates admitted Ka-Zar without hesitation to the palace. He needed no escort to find his way to Zut's quarters, the only ascetic chamber in that massive pile of decadent splendor.

His bare feet made no sound on the tiled floors of the long corridors and unannounced, he finally thrust aside the coarse draperies that curtained the door of the counselor's room.

A single glance showed him Zut and Seti, seated close together and engaged in earnest conversation. Letting the curtain drop silently back into place, Ka-Zar stepped back. Ever since the fiasco that he had made of the sacrifice to Pthos, he had avoided meeting the High Priest. And he had no desire to meet that repellent, obese creature now.

He lingered outside the portal, thinking that he would wait until Seti had finished his visit. Inside, the two men were speaking in low, hushed tones that carried to the curtain only in an indistinguishable murmur.

Indistinguishable, that is, to ordinary mortal ears. But Ka-Zar's ears were of the jungle—keen—delicately attuned to catch the faint murmur of a dying breeze, the thin hum of a mosquito, the barely audible hiss of a hidden snake. Standing outside in the dimming hall, he heard Seti's voice and he could distinctly make out the words.

". . . . . and I can no longer wait; I can no longer hold them."

"The time has come then," he heard Zut answer. "You have only to await my signal." He paused a moment as if considering. Then: "When the eternal flame burns crimson—strike!"

"Tomorrow." That was Seti, more urgent this time.

And after another brief pause, Zut echoed: "Very well. Tomorrow."

Though the conversation was at once recorded indelibly on Ka-Zar's brain, it held no meaning for him. Hearing the scrape of feet and knowing that the visit of the High Priest had ended, he moved a few yards further on down the hall, stepped back into a shadowy recess in the wall.

He waited until the figure of Seti appeared, waddled out of sight in the opposite direction. After the High Priest had gone but before he stepped out of his hiding place, Ka-Zar heard the harsh but muffled sound of a brazen gong in Zut's chamber.

For some inexplicable reason he stayed where he was, watching. His instinct was rewarded when a moment later a black shadow materialized soundlessly from nowhere. The lamps set in the brackets upon the walls had not yet been lit. A gray, obscure twilight filled the halls but Ka-Zar's slitted eyes recognized the moving shadow as one of the black slaves, taller and more powerfully built than his stunted fellows. Silently he watched the man dart a quick glance to right and to left, then vanish through the curtains into Zut's chamber.

That something was afoot was now evident. This time Ka-Zar approached the portal very deliberately and very cautiously, laid one ear against the curtain and listened.

It was well that he did, for the words that drifted out to him were very startling, indeed.

"Zoab," Zut addressed his surreptitious caller, "I have a task for you— a very, very dangerous task."

"My master has but to speak," answered the slave.

"Very well, then. Ask me no question and if you value your life, breathe no word of what I tell you. Find your brother Mu and bind him to the same secrecy. Tonight, at midnight I shall admit you both to the palace by the north gate. Make your way swiftly and silently to the Queen's bedchamber. A single thrust of a dagger as she sleeps—that is all."

KA-ZAR heard the slave's sharp intake of breath, realized that for an instant his own heart had stopped breathing.

"It shall be done," came Zoab's low voice.

"Yours shall be the hand of destiny," murmured Zut.

Again Ka-Zar glided noiselessly away from the door, melted into the shadows as Zoab appeared and swiftly vanished again. His own brain reeled. Now for the first time he remembered the growing tension of the people of Khalli. Something dark and dire was brewing. But the murder of the Queen . . . .

His face was thoughtful when at last he pushed aside the curtains and entered Zut's meagrely furnished quarters. His enigmatical mentor greeted him in friendly but absent-minded fashion. Ka-Zar returned the greeting as briefly, squatted as always in jungle fashion on his haunches.

For long moments each was busy with his own thoughts. Both were dwelling on the scenes that had just transpired, but each from a different angle.

To Zut, the message that Seti had brought him had been dark tidings. Zut realized that he and the High Priest had done their work too well—they had stirred the blacks up to revolt, stirred them up too far. In his wisdom Zut knew that he was no longer safe, that when the deluge broke, he could not stem it. And so though he had given his word to give the fateful signal the following day, he had no intention of signing what would prove to be his own death warrant. No. He would strike tonight. With Tamiris slain, he would

seize the reins of power. With the Queen they had been taught to hate removed—with this favorite of the gods, of his own creating, who now sat before him—he would be able to control them.

Ka-Zar, too, was thinking deeply. Though he could find only hate in his heart for the she-leopard who ruled these Oman, he was strangely disturbed. For the first time he felt the beginnings of a vague distrust for this man who had been his friend and mentor. To strike in the dark—to slay without warning one who was unarmed and defenseless—that was not Ka-Zar's way.

Forgetting w h a t h a d originally brought him there, and not caring to voice his troubled thought, he rose at last, spoke a few idle words and took his leave.

Once more out in the hall, he hesitated. Then on the spur of a sudden impulse, instead of leaving the palace, he turned and sought a hiding place instead.

A few moments later attendants came with tapers and soon the palace was a blaze of light. But none dreamed that within its walls, unseen, unheard, the jungle giant waited for the coming of midnight.

CHAPTER XIII

Death Comes Creeping

THE windows of Queen Tamiris' bedchamber were opened wide to the warm night air. An enormous, swollen globe of a moon hung low over the Congo, sent its effulgent-light streaming in broad bands through the aperture. The mellow moonlight picked out the pattern of the rugs, glistened from the steps of a low dais, bathed a silken-covered couch and the still form that lay upon it.

A tall screen of paper made from papyrus threw a dense black shadow in one corner of the room. And in that patch of blackness, only a pair of glowing, amber eyes betrayed the fact that Ka-Zar kept his vigil. He had stolen into the chamber as silently as the moonbeams themselves and now not even the sound of his hushed breathing disturbed the youthful Queen in her slumbers.

In profound meditation he stared at her. The night was sultry and she had flung aside the covers of the couch. All her tinkling ornaments had been discarded. A sheer robe of cobwebs and delicate in color as the first blush of dawn, swathed her slender figure. Her raven hair spread across her pillow and her eyes were closed.

In repose, all the harshness, all the arrogance was gone from her features. In the magic alchemy of the moonlight she appeared but the child that she really was—frail, helpless, innocent, virginal. And Ka-Zar, watching, was strangely perturbed. All the hate melted from his heart and a protecting tenderness crept into it instead.

It was no sound that roused him from his reverie. It was, rather, some sixth jungle sense that stirred the hairs at the nape of his neck. His head jerked around and he stared off to his right.

In the dimness beyond the brilliant bars of moonlight, a solid black shadow took form. Then another.

Ka-Zar tensed as the twin dark blotches stole soundlessly forward toward the royal couch. The course of the assassins would bring them past his own hiding place.

He crouched; his huge hands opened. Nerves on edge, he waited.

Zoab was in the lead. There was the subdued glint of bared steel in his hand. He moved forward slowly—one step—another—then another. Gathering his muscles, Ka-Zar sprang.

A bronzed arm wrapped itself about Zoab's body, tightened like a vise. A sinewy forearm slid under his chin, jerked it violently back. There was a faint but ominous *snap*. The blade slipped from Zoab's hand and dropped noiselessly onto the deep-piled rug underfoot.

With only a tiny, sibilant sigh whistling from his lips, his neck broken, Zoab collapsed in the arms of the jungle giant.

Ka-Zar let the lifeless body slump to the rug as he whirled to confront his victim's brother. Mu's eyes glittered in the darkness as he bounded forward, a wicked-looking dagger in his upraised hand. With a strangled snarl, the second black aimed full at Ka-Zar's bare chest.

The gleaming point descended in a swift downward arc. Then it was arrested in mid-air as Ka-Zar's hand flashed out, clamped about the wrist of the black. A single deft, powerful twist and the course of the hungry blade was deflected. Still carried by the momentum of the original stroke, it swooped down, bit avidly into the soft flesh at the base of Mu's throat.

Warm crimson spurted in its wake. The knees of the traitorous slave buckled. The life poured from his body as he stood swaying on his feet. Then, a sodden corpse that would never move again, he collapsed over the body of his brother.

The whole incident had transpired swiftly and with hardly a sound. Like a great shadow, Ka-Zar melted into the blackness once more and vanished, leaving the Queen's bedchamber in possession of the mellow moonlight and two dark, sinister objects that had not been there a few short moments before.

KA-ZAR did not know that Tamiris had been sleeping lightly. He did not know that had her fringe of dark lashes had lifted just in time for her to witness the silent struggle. There was no mistaking the terrible purpose of these two armed slaves. But before she could stir or cry out, she had seen them meet their fate. And she had recognized, in the dimness of the room, the brawny form of the bronzed giant who had outwitted them.

As he disappeared, with mingled emotions she rose from her couch, crossed the room and stared down at the lifeless bodies on the floor, at the spreading blotch of crimson that stained the rug. She was shaken by the narrowness of her escape; grave, as she realized the far-reaching significance of this treacherous attempt to slay her. The fact that Ka-Zar—who had openly defied and scorned her—had saved her life, was something to marvel and puzzle over.

He had not lingered to receive her thanks, apparently he had not even wished to be recognized. What then, was his motive in thus risking his life for one he scorned?

Tamiris could not guess. To her, the only thing that was obvious was that the strange jungle giant, for some reasons of his own, did not wish his midnight exploit to be known. And therefore, summoning her most trusted slaves and binding them to secrecy, she bade them remove the bodies and dispose of them with the utmost caution.

There was no more sleep for the Queen that night. Morning found her still pondering the fact that her throne was trembling upon its foundations, that a dire crisis was approaching in the affairs of Khalli. Digging the painted nails of her hands into her palms, she reminded herself that she was the daughter of the Ptolemies.

She lashed herself to a rage against these degenerate blacks who dared to threaten her, worked herself up into a fury against the scheming Zut. Some-how she sensed that he was behind the attack of the night before. The crafty counsellor was avaricious for power. He would go to any lengths to attain it.

Once, in a moment of weakness, unwanted and unaccustomed tears welled suddenly to the eyes of the youthful Queen. She flung herself on a divan and buried her burning face in her ivory hands. All the attributes of her sovereignty, all the hard shell that she had imposed upon herself, slipped away. She became her natural self—a young girl alone and lonesome and apprehensive for the future.

If only—she mused bitterly—she but had a real man to fight by her side. A man she could trust. And with the thought the inscrutable amber eyes of Ka-Zar blazed once more before her.

The breath caught in her throat. The tears ceased miraculously and with intent and burning eyes she straightened slowly on the divan.

Those eyes had surveyed her with scorn, with mockery, with contempt—true. But they were honest eyes, fearless ones—innocent of the faintest breath of treachery or deceit. Daughter of kings for ten thousand years, Tamiris was the end product of a super-civilization. And now she sensed that the same heritage of royal blood flowed through the veins of this jungle god.

God indeed! He had dominance over the savage beasts of the wilderness; he had dominance over men, both black and white. Tamiris' pulse beat faster and twin spots of color blazed in her cheeks. Swiftly jumping from the divan she crossed the room to an ebony chest, inlaid with mother-of-pearl. Lifting up the lid she picked up a gem-encrusted mirror and holding it before her flushed face, she gazed at her reflection for a long time.

Then with a sudden, impetuous movement, she flung the mirror from her.

"Yes," she whispered dramatically.

"And he has dominance over you, Tamiris! I read it in your eyes!"

Her turbulent young heart became a welter of seething and conflicting emotions. For a long time she struggled with herself, fought with her pride—and lost. She told herself that it was a matter of state business that made her clap her hands and bring her slaves and maids running to serve her.

"Go," she said imperiously to one, "find this Ka-Zar. Tell him that the Queen desires him to attend her at once."

Then as the black scurried off, she turned to her maids. "My finest jewels—my most resplendent garments. Hurry—a scented bath—my hair. . . ."

KA-ZAR received her summons with a grunt that did not betray his emotions. A scowl made a deep V between his brows and his eyes darkened. What did this disturbing Queen want of him now? He longed only to be free of the encroaching confines of this outlandish city, longed to be many moons journey away in the distant forest that was his home. His jungle called him. What of Trajah the elephant and Sha the lioness? How fared Zar's cubs and Nono's brothers? What was transpiring in his wilderness domain? A shadow crossed his mind and his tawny eyes became hard. During his long absence, had any intruder come to violate the sanctity of the jungle?

Very well. He would see this barbaric queen. Then he would not rest until he had found a means of escape from this lost kingdom.

He met Zut as he walked through the halls of the palace. Zut stroked his greasy beard with a skinny hand. "The Queen has sent for you, Son of Pthos?" he asked.

Ka-Zar answered with a growl of assent.

Zut did not know that the bronze man before him had foiled his dastardly attempt on the life of the Queen. He was still sorely mystified and much upset by the fact that the plot had somehow miscarried and his trusted emissaries had failed to return. Matters were coming fast to a climax. He might need this jungle god and he did not like this summons of the Queen.

"Beware the wiles and snares of a woman," he whined. "Honey can drip from the tongue of Tamiris even as she weaves plots like a crafty spider weaves its web."

Ka-Zar's nostrils flared. His new mistrust of this old schemer grew in his heart. The whining voice sickened him.

"You speak with the voice of the jackal," he retorted. "Or in the manner of Sinassa the snake who crawls upon his belly. This Queen is but a woman—the female of her species—to be mastered like any other."

Zut shrugged. "Rash words, my son, spoken bravely but in ignorance. The enmity of Tamiris, once aroused, is not to be scorned. Her craving for power holds nothing sacred. Did you know that the old king, her father, died of a mysterious gnawing of his vitals? Yet during the days of his illness, all his food and drink were prepared only by the hands of his daughter."

With the terrible insinuation ringing in his ears, Ka-Zar turned on his heel and with his mind in a turmoil, he headed for the Queen's apartments.

CHAPTER XIV

The Queen Commands

AT his entrance, Tamiris dismissed her maids. They had done their work swiftly and well. Her body was oiled and perfumed. An elaborate headdress of sapphires and emeralds, formed in the shape of the Sphinx, crowned her sleek hair. The precious stuff that sheathed her slim hips was of iridescent blues and greens. Every inch of her semi-nude body was covered with glinting jewels.

She was proud, striking, as a peacock in her dazzling finery—and beautiful beyond mortal dreams. Ka-Zar stopped short, confronted her squarely and unabashed, boldly appraised her.

A delicate flush mantled Tamiris' ivory cheeks and her heart beat with a dull pounding against the jeweled discs that covered her breasts. But equally unabashed, unashamed, she let his eyes drink their fill. Royalty was meeting royalty on an equal footing. And if Tamiris was feminine loveliness incarnate, Ka-Zar was the most magnificent specimen of manhood she had ever seen.

She raised her hand at last and as Ka-Zar strode forward, she rose to greet him.

"The Queen welcomes you, Son of Pthos," she said in her low, husky voice.

At the mention of the god of darkness, a scowl descended on Ka-Zar's face. "Your Pthos means nothing to me," he said evenly. "I am of the jungle where only the sun is god."

Tamiris drew herself up to her full height. "I, too, am a Daughter of the Sun. And on that common ground, we shall talk."

"Ka-Zar listens," he answered noncommittally.

"Very well. Hear then. Troublous times have come to Khalli. At any moment my kingdom will be torn by uprising and revolt. The degenerate slaves, under the evil banner of Pthos and under the leadership of the scheming Zut, will attempt to wrest Khalli from the true followers of Isis. It will be a combat between the forces of evil and the forces of justice and right.

"By some miracle the gods have sent you, king of the jungle, to my country. Was it really Pthos—were you destined to aid the powers of darkness? I cannot believe it. You cannot escape— you must make your choice. Your eyes are fearless and honest. I can only believe that you belong to the side of right."

For a long moment Ka-Zar did not answer. Tamiris sounded sincere, the passion with which she spoke was genuine. Was this what Zut meant? Was this more of her artful deceit? Was she daring to make a fool of him?

With keen feminine intuition, Tamiris guessed his thoughts.

"Zut has told you evil of me. Is it not so?"

Ka-Zar did not speak.

"Answer!" she commanded.

"It is so," he challenged, his eyes level.

The Queen's face paled. "And you believed?" she asked huskily.

"Ka-Zar has eyes to see."

"Yet Ka-Zar is blind."

"Ka-Zar knows that it was you who had him chained by the neck to the pillar of stone."

Tamiris bit her scarlet underlip, then confronted him unflinchingly. "In your jungle, O Ka-Zar, there is but one law —the law of survival. It is the same here in Khalliland. I, too, must obey it. That law is greater than you or me. You are a man grown but your heart is simple and your mind is that of a child." She stepped closer to him and a passionate earnestness and pleading came into her voice. "Believe not the tales concerning me with which Zut has poisoned your mind. Zut is evil."

"Yet he of all in Khalli befriended me," answered Ka-Zar stubbornly.

Tamiris stamped her regal, sandaled foot. "Fool!" she burst out impetuously. "For his own evil ends. He sees that you have power over the blacks. They fear you—worship you.

Zut would use you like bait in a trap. And then when he has accomplished his dark ends, he would discard you. Cast you to the prowling jackals."

AT her words, anger swelled the veins in Ka-Zar's throat. But he did not know whether that anger was directed at the girl or at Zut.

Tamiris was quick to see his confusion and pressed her advantage. "Zut is a traitor. His tongue drips with lies. He is black of heart. My father died of some slow, insidious poison. Yet the only poison known in Khalli is the bitter waters of the underground spring, that kills swiftly and surely.

"Tamiris has no proof. Zut is the direct descendant of Egyptian magicians. Somehow the black arts have been passed down secretly through the generations and he possesses strange, dark knowledge of which we others know not. My father's death was a lingering one. Zut did not believe that in my youth, I would dare to challenge him. He thought to usurp my throne and now his thwarted ambition will not let him rest."

Her words only confused Ka-Zar the more. His simple mind was not fitted to cope with such intrigues, with such plot and counter-plot. Zut had just insinuated that Tamiris had murdered her own father. Now she claimed that the counsellor was the true murderer.

If she was telling the truth, Ka-Zar could understand much, forgive all she had done to him. For his own father had been murdered by a covetous white man.

Now Tamiris laid bare her heart. With the humility of a woman and the pride of a Queen, with her chin held high and in her eyes a melting appeal, she spoke in low but steady tones.

"You have scorned Tamiris and mocked her. You have confounded all her plans and been the cause of her undoing. Yet she has searched her soul and found not hate, but love for you. Even the Daughter of the Sun is but a woman, with all a woman's weakness.

"Smile upon me, Lord of the jungle. Take your place by my side. Together we shall rule Khalli. Together we shall quell our enemies and reign, a royal and truly-mated pair, upon my now lonely throne."

Ka-Zar could scarce believe his ears. With wide eyes he gazed at the girl who stood proud and unashamed before him, laying her heart and her throne at his feet. Suddenly he realized that since the night before, the vision that had tormented him both day and night had been banished forever. The laughing blue eyes and sunny hair of Claudette had been blotted out by eyes of midnight blackness, by hair as sleek and blue-black as the raven's wing.

It was the sight of her, as he had watched her the night before, that had worked some subtle magic. He had seen her then unadorned, slim and virginal. Now she faced him in all the glory of her love, perfumed, glittering, alluring, utterly desirable.

A fever possessed him. His blood pounded through his veins, set a pulse throbbing at his temples. The exquisite face of this barbaric Queen swam before his eyes. His brain reeled. The thought of taking her for his mate set every fibre of his being aquiver.

A rare confusion assailed him. In sheer panic, without speaking a word, he turned and fled from her presence.

Dazed, rooted to the spot, the Queen stood and watched him vanish. Her bosom rose and fell once convulsively. Her tiny hands clenched at her sides. It was beyond belief. She—a daughter of the Ptolemies—had offered her heart to this naked, jungle savage. And instead of prostrating himself at her feet—he had gone without a word!

For a moment she trembled under the lash of outraged pride. Then suddenly she flung herself upon the divan, buried her hot face in her arms. A single bitter tear squeezed through her lids and made a darker blotch upon a silken cushion.

BLINDLY Ka-Zar fled the palace. His soul was in a turmoil. Without aim or purpose he wandered through the narrow streets of the city. Vaguely he was aware that the people he passed seemed equally perturbed. Each looked askance at the other. Fear and mistrust was written on every face. Little groups gathered in doorways to talk in hushed whispers, fell silent as he stalked past.

Twilight fell at last, bringing with it no relief. The oppressive heat of the day became a sultry night. Still Ka-Zar prowled restlessly through crooked alleys, wandered like a lost soul up and down endless flights of hewn stone steps.

The Egyptian inhabitants retired into their houses at an early hour that night, barring their doors behind them. By the time the huge golden moon came up over the rim of the cliffs, the streets of the city were deserted.

Not till then did Ka-Zar's brain clear a trifle. Not till then did his mind hark back to the day before, not till then did he recall Zut's promise to Seti.

"When the flame burns crimson— strike!"

The words could only refer to one thing. Unconsciously Ka-Zar's glance traveled upward, came to rest on the pillar of flame that rose in a steady shaft from the topmost tier of the city, far above him.

Now he realized the full, terrible import of that signal. And with sudden dismay he realized that at any moment he might see the eternal light suddenly change to a glowing crimson.

There was no time to question why he should be so appalled at the thought. With one stroke he wiped from his mind all the thousand and one conflicting thoughts that had harassed him. Then with but a single, clear-cut purpose, he made all speed toward the top of the city.

In the same manner that Chaka the great ape swung through the trees of the jungle, Ka-Zar scaled the ramparts of Khalli. With the sure-footedness of the antelope he ran lightly across the rim of the walls, hardly conscious of the perilous depths below. With leaps a leopard might have envied, he went ever upward.

At last, panting, he gained the topmost terrace of the city. He found it to be a luxuriant hanging garden, a rectangular plot of swaying palms, dripping orchids, splashing fountains. From its center rose a sheer-sided pylon built of clay bricks. It was from the top of this pylon that the eternal flame flung its steady banner skyward.

The moonlight and the pillar of fire overhead checkered the gardens with patches of brilliant light and alternate patches of Stygian shadow under the spreading palms.

Ka-Zar had arrived with not a moment to spare. Even as he flung himself over the wall and dropped nimbly to the ground, he saw a black figure dart across the garden, scale nimbly up the side of the pylon. With a low growl rumbling in his throat, he sprinted off in hot pursuit.

With all the agility of Nono the monkey, despite his massive body, he climbed up the slanting pile of clay bricks. Each was recessed a half inch from the one below it and that was all the purchase that his fingers and bare toes needed.

He emerged on a narrow, bare platform. Apparently the pylon was hollow, for the mysterious flame issued from a hole in its center. The black stood balanced on straddled legs a scant few feet away. The light gleamed on the ebony skin of his upraised arms. Both his fists were clenched—he was about to throw something into the heart of the flame.

He never completed the movement. With a low snarl Ka-Zar flung himself upon him and an instant later they were locked in a death-grip.

It was a silent, atavistic struggle that transpired there up on the topmost peak of the city. In vain the black struggled to free himself of the giant's grip. They swayed back and forth, perilously close to the edge of the pylon. But the black was no match for the mighty man of bronze. Suddenly he was plucked from his foothold, raised high on powerful arms.

KICKING and struggling in a frenzy of fear, the helpless black guessed Ka-Zar's intention. But he could do nothing. Even as a shrill wail of terror tore from his lips, he was hurled through the air as though he had been shot from a catapult. His body turned over and over as he flew far out over the walls, then plunged precipitately downward.

He vanished from his victor's sight. Then his last frenzied shriek, cut off abruptly, floated back to tell that he had been smashed on the rocks far below.

Atop the pylon, the glowing flame shimmering on his naked bronze body, Ka-Zar looked out over the valley toward the distant caverns. Over there, many eyes were watching, awaiting the crimson signal that would unleash bloody war in Khalli. Flinging back his head, squaring his brawny shoulders, he sent the thundering roar of the lion floating across the sultry air.

As the cliffs picked up his cry of defiance and sent it echoing back and forth across the valley, with the back of his hand Ka-Zar mopped the great beads of sweat that bedewed his brow. A fine black powder had spilled from the hands of the black. It strewed the top of the pylon; it made daubs on his sweat-streaked body. Carefully he blew it off the clay bricks, away from the steady-burning flame; rubbed it off his flesh. Then he lowered himself over the edge of the platform and climbed down the side of the pylon.

As he retraced his way through the dappled stretches of the gardens, he realized that once again he had impulsively foiled Zut's plans. He determined to seek out the counsellor, speak out openly, try to get at the real truth hidden in the network of lies, suspicions and intrigues in which he was caught like an insect in a spider's web. That he must take a hand in the coming clash, on one side or the other, was now inescapable. Perhaps a talk with Zut would help him to make up his mind, help him to decide once and for all which way he should choose.

CHAPTER XV
Delivered Unto Pthos

KA-ZAR wasted much time in Khalli trying to find Zut, only to learn at last that directly after the cry of the lion had floated down from the top of the pylon, Zut had betaken himself hurriedly toward the underground habitations on the other side of the valley.

Ka-Zar started off in the same direction.

He was halfway down the long, dim jungle road when a great black shadow materialized from the brush at one side of the road and Zar padded silently into place beside him. Nono dropped down from a branch, climbed swiftly up onto his master's shoulder.

Ka-Zar dropped a hand onto the tawny head of his brother. "Like Sinassa the snake, trouble rears its ugly head in the valley," he told Zar in the guttural language of the jungle. "Soon there will be much fighting and bloodshed. Lie low here in the jungle. If Ka-Zar needs you, he will call."

Zar did not understand why his two-legged brother must share the doings of these hated Oman. Yet if he must, he would fain go by his side.

But Ka-Zar was adamant. And at last Zar, bowing to a wisdom greater than his own but with his heart filled with gloomy forebodings, faded once more into the underbrush. Ka-Zar tried to loosen Nono's grip about his neck, told the silly creature to scamper off into the safety of the forest. But Nono clung tighter and chattered his protest. The little monkey's eyes were filled with such pleading that Ka-Zar finally shrugged and permitted him to remain.

Once he had left the forest and plunged into the dark caverns under the cliffs, a slave told him that he would find Zut at the Temple of Pthos. Again Ka-Zar had to overcome his old aversion to the dim chamber with its monstrous, leering god.

He found his way surely and swiftly around the edge of the lake. All along the route he passed groups of muttering blacks. Each time they prostrated themselves before him, gazed in the same awe and wonder at this bronze giant with the little monkey atop his shoulder. As Ka-Zar turned into the passageway, there was barely room for him to pass. The tunnel was jammed with a throng of blacks, keeping a respectful distance away from Zut and Seti who were speaking earnestly together before the bronze door of the temple.

The animated conversation of the counsellor and the High Priest died abruptly as the tall form of Ka-Zar approached them. Zut's face, with its skin of wrinkled old parchment, betrayed no sign of emotion. Yet at the sight of his naked bronze disciple a slow fury smouldered in his breast. The wily counsellor's schemes had availed him nought. The plot on the life of the Queen had failed and he had been obliged to keep his promise to Seti, taking the chance that he might somehow survive the holocaust. Yet the signal had not been given—and the roar of the lion echoing out from the top of the city had told him why. It explained, also, why Zoab and Mu had never returned.

Zut turned to confront Ka-Zar. His fingers clawed at his beard. "So—you did not heed my warning," he accused. "You listened to the lying words of the Queen—listened and like an utter fool, believed. You call yourself a man. Bah! You are a weakling—a lump of clay in the hands of a woman!"

Had he weighed his words carefully for days, Zut could have found no taunt more sure to rouse Ka-Zar's wrath. This insult stabbed him to the quick and a swift retort came to his lips.

"Zut is angry only because he wishes me to be clay in his own hands," he answered hotly. "Zut speaks of being a man. Is he a man who plots in the dark, who sends others with knives to slay a defenseless woman?"

ZUT did not know that Ka-Zar was still undecided, that he had come seeking him in a last desperate effort to make up his own mind about the justice and right in this matter which had split up the kingdom. Zut did see, though, the swift suspicion that glinted in Seti's eyes as he heard Ka-Zar's last words. This wild man of the jungle was causing much trouble and something would have to be done immediately, lest he menace Zut's very life.

The last tattered remnants of the

cloak of friendship dropped from the counsellor. He drew his skinny form erect and his hawk-eyes glittered beneath his craggy brows.

"Very well, then," he said. "It matters not what an ignorant savage thinks of Zut. It was I who made a fool of you. I lied to you for my own ends, but I do not need you after all. It was I who poisoned the old king. I was the real ruler of Khalli, and though now this chit of a girl dares to defy me, I shall yet be the ruler in name as well as fact."

He whirled on the mob of blacks who crowded in the passage. Stretching forth a scrawny arm, he pointed a bony finger at Ka-Zar. "This man is a traitor!" he denounced. "It was he who blocked the giving of the signal. And now he dares to defy us in our own stronghold!"

The blacks gasped, stared back open-mouthed. In the long centuries of primitive cave-life, their brains had degenerated along with their bodies. They were too dull-witted to understand Zut's sudden change of heart. They had been taught to venerate Ka-Zar as god and now Zut called him a traitor.

Ka-Zar saw the blank, stupid faces of the blacks. He realized that though his fate hung once more in their hands, that without a leader to point the way, they were incapable of making any decision. And with that realization, he found the answer to the question that had been so long troubling him. For centuries these blacks had grubbed meekly away in their caves. The spark of rebellion had been planted in their dull wits by some unscrupulous, keener brain than their own. It was Zut, with the aid of Seti, who had stirred up this devil's brew in Khalli.

Zut saw the hesitation of the slaves, remembered with growing fury that he himself was responsible for the false miracle that had spared Ka-Zar. Such an idea once implanted in those thick skulls was not quickly dispelled. One false move and they might turn upon Zut and rend him. He had a sudden inspiration.

"This man is a traitor!" he cried again. "Zut denounces him—but Zut does not ask you to believe the word of a mortal man. If this Ka-Zar has dared to commit treason against the god who has protected and befriended him— that god alone will sit in judgment on him. Throw him into the Temple of Pthos—leave him alone to face his god. At sunrise you will find whether Zut has spoken the truth."

Seti's doughy face quivered. Echoing Zut's thundering accusation with a torrent of high, shrill words, he waddled to the door, flung the portal open.

His movement broke the spell that held the blacks. Like automatons, with harsh cries, they surged down the passage. At the sight of the horde rushing at him, Ka-Zar held his ground. But the little monkey squeaked in terror, dropped from his perch and with fearful glances over his shoulder at the oncoming blacks, scampered blindly in the opposite direction.

In vain Ka-Zar braced himself—in vain he lashed out as the first slaves charged at him. There was no stemming that leaping, shouting, black tide. Ka-Zar was almost lifted from his feet, rushed through the open doorway and hurled with terrific force into the Temple of Pthos. The bronze door slammed behind him with a crash like the knell of doom.

CHAPTER XVI

THE IDOL IS SMASHED

KA-ZAR smashed heavily into the far wall, spun around with the spitting scream of N'Jagi ringing in his ears. Instinctively his hand whipped to his belt for the blade of steel that had always hung there. Then with a bitter laugh he realized that it was a long time since the blacks had taken his knife from him, on that first fateful night here in this very temple. Head crouched low between his shoulders, his body weaving slowly from side to side, bare-handed he set himself for the leopard's spring.

But almost to his disappointment, N'Jagi's black body did not plunge down upon him. Again the shrill scream of the beast echoed through the vaulted temple, followed by the clink of a metal chain.

His narrowed eyes orbing the semi-darkness, Ka-Zar looked up to the narrow ledge that extended over the door. Gleaming opals of hate glared down at him. And there, straining against the chains that held him fast to the wall was N'Jagi.

His fangs were bared; his gaping jaws slavered. A strange, unearthly cry issued from his throat as with frustrated rage he threw his weight against his chain.

Arms akimbo, Ka-Zar rocked back on his heels and laughed up at the leopard. "So, N'Jagi," he taunted in the guttural language of the beasts. "Your master the evil Zut fears for your life, so he chains you in safety."

At his mocking voice the devil was aroused again in the leopard. Once more his scream split the silence; once more he crouched back, then flung himself forward.

"Fool!" said Ka-Zar. "Break the chain, O N'Jagi—and you surely die."

Then with a show of utter disdain and contempt he turned his back on the snarling beast and swiftly surveyed the temple. He had been put into the Temple of Pthos to die, he knew. But if not before the sabre claws of N'Jagi —then by what dark agency? More trickery, this? More evil cunning of the bloodthirsty Oman?

Then slowly, as if impelled by some irresistible fascination his eyes were drawn to the hideous idol of the god that stood upon the dais. Again all its malignant evil assailed him like a living thing. The flesh crawled on his back; he bared his teeth. Then he flung back his head and sent the challenging roar of the lion crashing through the dim chamber.

The hated cry lashed N'Jagi to a new outburst of demoniacal fury.

Ka-Zar ignored the leopard, concentrated his suddenly narrowed eyes on the idol. Some sixth psychic sense told him that whatever the danger that threatened him, it was represented by that hideous image of stone.

All the dark tales he had heard concerning it came crowding back to him. It was evil. It demanded human sacrifice. Its appetite was insatiable. Once a victim had been delivered up to Pthos, he was never seen again.

Ka-Zar knew that he was intended as such a victim. But though the idol held him with a dread fascination, he feared it not. Pthos to him was but a name. He knew naught about gods, good or evil—and he cared less. He trusted in the might of his own right arm and in his friends, the jungle creatures.

Spells, magic, terrible curses—Bah! He took a long challenging step forward towards the idol. A thing of stone could not hurt him!

True.

But the thing behind that thing of stone could slay him! The hideous and grinning face of the idol concealed a second face equally as repulsive. The only difference between them was that this second one, instead of being carved from stone, was compounded of living flesh and blood and bone.

IT was the face of Zut—evil, passion-distorted. To his pursed thin lips he held a short reed pipe that jutted an inch through one of the holes that made the idol's sightless eyes. And quivering at the end of that pipe was a tiny, poisoned dart. No man in all Khalli save Zut knew the secret of that poison —knew that it struck swifter than the poison of the burning well and left no tell-tale trace behind.

That was the dread secret of the idol of Pthos. It was hollow. And now crouched behind it, squinting through its gaping eye-socket, Zut expanded his lungs and waited for his victim to approach closer.

The blood pounded swiftly through Ka-Zar's veins and though beads of sweat popped out on his brow, he felt cold and numb and strangely apprehensive. His nostrils flared to the scent of danger; every nerve and sense flashed a shrill warning to his brain.

Instinct told him that danger lay before him. And he met it in the only way he knew how—by advancing. The stony face of the idol held him fascinated. It was a form of hypnotism.

And so intent was he on the leering face of the image—so intent was Zut on his steady approach—that neither saw the rapidly moving blur of shadow that scurried across a narrow ledge on the rear wall, then dropped agilely to the dais.

Zut's lips were pursued around the mouth of the blowpipe; his lungs were expanded to the full. Squinting through the narrow aperture in the idol he drew a deadly bead on the base of the bronzed column of Ka-Zar's throat,

that loomed ever larger below him. He could not miss. He had done the self-same thing a score of times before and never once had he had such a splendid target.

Already in his mind's eye he saw the sudden recoil of the jungle giant as the poisoned barb sank home; saw him shudder convulsively, claw at his throat, then sink to the ground. So the jungle god had fallen for a woman's wiles. Fool! He could have ruled in Khalli along with Zut.

Now, instead, he would fall victim to the very hungry Pthos!

He tongued the mouth of the reed—expanded his lungs—he . . .

There was a sudden hiss behind him —a patter of running feet—then needle-like claws dug deep into his spine and a pair of long and spidery arms wrapped themselves around his neck.

The impact of the unexpected weight on his back deflated the air in Zut's lungs—and spoiled his aim. The poisoned dart whizzed from the blow-pipe, whined angrily past Ka-Zar's ear.

From behind the grinning idol and muffled by it came a guttural curse, followed by a furious, scolding chatter. Ka-Zar recognized both sounds. The first was human and he would have sworn that that familiar chatter came from no other than Nono the silly one.

He leaped forward. With one mighty spring he bounded up onto the platform. Three long strides took him to the rear of the idol. And there, gray of face, stark fear in his eyes, Zut vainly essayed to choke the life from the monkey with one hand, while he wrenched at the dagger at his belt with the other. He never succeeded in either attempt.

With a guttural snarl Ka-Zar leaped in. The steel fingers of his right hand closed around Zut's scrawny neck, as the momentum of his charge flung the Egyptian back against the cold body of the idol.

ZUT dropped the whimpering monkey as his dagger cleared his belt. But long before he could whip it up Ka-Zar had caught his wrist in a grip of steel. As if it were but a green twig, Zut's arm bent back beneath the jungle giant's pressure. He winced, he cried out in agony—he screamed and the dagger fell to the floor with a metallic clang.

His cries of agony, however, were drowned in the hideous screams of N'Jagi as the black leopard, fangs gnashing wracked his sleek body against the chain that held him.

For once Zut had been too sure of himself. He had overplayed his hand.

Powerful arms swept him from his feet, held him high aloft above the idol's head. Looking down into the implacable tawny eyes of Ka-Zar, Zut read the fate that was in store for him. Instead of being the executioner, he was to be the victim that was to satisfy the blood lust of the unholy Pthos. In another moment his skull would be crushed like a rotten gourd against the stony face of the idol.

In that moment the Machiavellian Zut begged for his life. "Hold, Oh Ka-Zar," he pleaded. "Forget not that it was Zut who gave you the antidote to the poison cup of the Queen."

Ka-Zar's mighty limbs trembled with the hate that was upon him. Yet what the crawling thing in his hands had said was true. His eyes smouldered. "You tricked me," he said. "You have fed me with lies."

"Yet forget not that it was I who saved you," quavered Zut.

"Ka-Zar does not forget," said the jungle giant. "A life for a life. I give you back yours, now."

He suddenly lowered the trembling figure to his hip. Then implanting the sole of his bare foot high up on the base of the idol, he heaved mightily. The stone image trembled, groaned, loosed on its moorings. Then, with a final thrust, Ka-Zar sent it crashing down from the dais to the hard floor of the temple, where it broke into a dozen pieces.

Directly behind where the idol had stood, a small section of the masonry jutted out from the wall. It had been cunningly fashioned and hinged, this secret aperture and it explained how Zut had so mysteriously gained his devilish place of concealment.

The crash of the toppled idol was still rumbling in the vaulted temple, when Ka-Zar threw back the bronze door and stood silhouetted for a moment in the doorway. High above his head at arms' length he held the trembling Zut. Below him, their startled and terror-stricken faces lit up by the weird lights from a score of torches, Seti and his followers fell back.

A howl of consternation rose from their wolfish lips. They would have been less startled if the stone image of Pthos, itself, had appeared in the doorway. And before they could recover, Ka-Zar sent the screaming Zut hurtling down onto their heads.

The packed ranks of the slaves wavered, broke. Even the flaming torches were knocked from their brackets as the mob fled. And when Seti managed at last to recover one and to hold it aloft the temple door was empty.

Ka-Zar had vanished.

CHAPTER XVII

First Blood

THREE minutes later his towering form leaped through the main gate to the City of Khalli. The sleepy sentrys on duty there, looked up with wide eyes at his precipitate entrance, grasped their spears more firmly.

Pulling to an abrupt halt, Ka-Zar spoke to them swiftly. "The gate! Close it at once!" he commanded.

The guards looked at him stupidly and impatient at the delay, Ka-Zar presented his broad shoulders to the massive gate and slowly swung it to. Not until the heavy bronze bar had been set securely in its place did he turn again to the guards.

"There will be dark trouble in Khalli, tonight," he said prophetically. "Dark trouble and much bloodshed. Spurred on by the treacherous Zut and Seti, the blacks are rising."

The faces of the sentries showed swift alarm.

"The gate to the city is to be opened to no one," continued Ka-Zar hurriedly. "Least of all to Zut. Mark my words well and if you fail you shall have Ka-Zar to reckon with. Blow thy horn, trumpeter! Arouse your men! Man the walls!"

He broke off abruptly as from somewhere far towards the south came a deep, ominous rumble, the distant clamor or angry voices.

"The slaves are already on the march," continued Ka-Zar. "Blow, trumpeter, blow! And if need be, let each man of you die tonight for your city and your Queen!"

The savage clamor of the approaching blacks rose louder in their ears. The trumpeter was paralyzed for a moment. Then he clapped his horn to his lips and blew three shrill blasts of alarm.

With the brazen notes still echoing back from the cliffs that hemmed in the city, Ka-Zar sped from the gate and made straight for Tamiris' palace.

He found the place in a confused turmoil as he brushed by the guard at the outer door. Men, rudely awakened from sleep, milled about in confusion as they buckled on their short swords. Others stared questioningly at one another and muttered a last prayer to the gods.

His bronzed figure towering above them, Ka-Zar commanded their attention with an upraised arm. "Men of Khalli," he called. "Hear me, hear me all. Led by the traitorous Zut and Seti, the black slaves have revolted. Even now they march on the inner city to slay and plunder—to slay your queen and to put the tyrant Zut upon the throne.

"To the walls, men of Khalli. Let your hearts be stout, your spears well aimed; and may the gods of Khalli lend strength to your sword arms."

His ringing words of challenge and defiance worked a miracle on the demoralized soldiers. They felt that they had in Ka-Zar an invincible ally—one favored by the gods. Their backs stiffened, their eyes glittered and shouting hoarse cries of alarm to the still sleeping city, they rushed from the palace and made for strategic positions on the walls.

When the last man han vanished, Ka-Zar sped across the now deserted entrance hall, leaped up the broad flight of marble steps at the far end, and without the formality of knocking entered Tamiris' apartment.

He found her dressed and waiting for him, surrounded by a handful of trembling maids. True, her face was slightly pale but her lips were resolute and there was no mark of fear upon her. Her eyes glowed with a steady, intense light and the while she fondly fingered the jeweled haft of the short dagger that hung from her girdle. . . .

Without waiting for an exchange of greetings she spoke. "Ka-Zar brings tidings?" she said.

"Dark tidings, O Tamiris," he answered. "The blacks have risen."

"I heard your words in the hall below," said the Queen. "And Ka-Zar—Lord of the jungle—does he fight or flee?"

KA-ZAR drew himself up to his full height and looked down for a long moment into her glowing eyes. Anger surged within him at her insinuating words. Then with a rush of sudden relief, he understood. Well might Tamiris be the daughter of an ancient civilization, but nevertheless, she was a true daughter of the jungle. In her own peculiar way she was spurring her mate onto battle, even as Sha might have done to Zar in defensive of their cubs.

"Ka-Zar—brother of the lion never flees from danger," he said. "Ka-Zar has come to fight—not for your city, not for your civilization, not for the men who call you Queen—but for you."

He laughed suddenly, swept her into his mighty arms, crushed her against his bronzed chest and kissed her fiercely.

Tamiris was breathless and bruised when he deposited her gently on her feet a moment later but in her heart was a great exultation. But before she could stay him, Ka-Zar was gone. And as the door clanged to behind his retreating back, a mighty shout went up from the walls and surrounded the city.

On his way out of the palace, Ka-Zar commandeered a long spear and a heavy, two-bladed sword. He balanced the first in his hand for a moment, then tested the blade of the other with his thumb. He found both to his satisfaction. His soul exulted and his heart beat swifter as once more he felt the weight and heft of weapons in his hands. For many moons, now, he had been unarmed. True, his bare fists were weapons enough against any dozen men in Khalli, be they white or black.

But now he was confronted by overwhelming hordes. Death would be swift. He determined to deal it more swiftly still.

When he reached the outer wall, he found the men of Khalli grim and alert at their posts. The dying moon glinted dully off spear head and broad sword. A mighty shout of welcome went up from the hosts that manned the wall.

Ka-Zar brandished his spear aloft in greeting, then swiftly surveyed the hurried scene of activity about him. A dozen paces back from the wall men sweated as they piled up huge mounds of stones beside strange looking devices. They looked to Ka-Zar like young trees of a dozen seasons' growth. One end of each was firmly implanted into the ground and attached to the other was a small platform of wood some two feet square.

Other groups of men bestirred themselves with bellows around a dozen fires. Over them, on iron bars, hung suspended as many steaming cauldrons of boiling water and oil. Ka-Zar had never seen such preparations before but shrewdly he guessed for what purpose the steaming liquid was to be used.

Outside, from beyond the wall, came a throaty, ominous rumble—the swelling guttural cries of a vast multitude.

Twenty paces from where he stood, Ka-Zar noted a group of men with their heads together in consultation. From their jeweled weapons and the purple of their robes he knew them to be chiefs—leaders of the white men of Khalli in time of emergency.

He hurried up to them and at his coming their teeth glinted brightly as they gave him welcome.

"I am Ankhamen," said a tall, patrician Egyptian. "It is my honor to command the Queen's men. In her name I welcome you to our ranks."

Ka-Zar smiled. "My spear is thirsty. My sword cries out for blood."

"Well spoken, O Ka-Zar, God of the jungle," said Ankhamen.

BUT the jungle giant shook his head. "Ka-Zar is no god. He is a man, even as you. He is here to fight. Once tonight he gave back to Zut his miserable life. He shall not spare him a second time. Why do not the blacks attack?"

"Zut has asked that we yield the city. He promises mercy. If not his hordes will storm the gate."

"And your answer?" asked Ka-Zar.

"We have been debating the issue."

Ka-Zar shook his head violently from side to side. "O foolish men of Khalli. Trust not the word of Zut or Seti. If you would answer, let your swords speak and your spears."

Ankhamen nodded in agreement. "Ka-Zar speaks with the tongue of wisdom. It shall be done as he says. I, myself, from the wall shall denounce the infamous Zut and Seti."

With the words he started for one of the flights of narrow stone steps that led to the top of the parapet.

Ka-Zar laid a heavy but gentle hand upon his arm and stayed him.

"You are old, Ankhamen," he said, his eyes shining with admiration. "Up there on the wall, a hurled javelin would be hard to dodge. And more, you are trusted of the Queen. She needs you. Let Ka-Zar speak to Zut and his followers. If they listen, all may be well. But if not, it shall be war."

So saying he turned abruptly, snatched a blazing torch from a soldier and crossed to the stone steps. He mounted them swiftly. Inside the wall all eyes followed his progress with breathless attention. Outside, the angry clamor rose to a frenzied din.

Awaiting the moment when the cries of the blacks had reached their peak, Ka-Zar suddenly leaped to the top of the parapet. High above his head he held the burning brand and the leaping tongues of flame bathed his bronzed body in rippling sheets of fire.

At the sudden appearance of the jungle god—the man who but a few short hours before had been considered by the slaves as the favored son of Pthos—the eternal symbol of light in one hand, a glinting spear in the other— a sudden hush fell over the packed ranks of the revolting legions.

For a long moment Ka-Zar stood there, straddle-legged on the parapet, motionless, immobile as if he had been carved from bronze. Only his slitted eyes were alive as they eagerly searched for the wizened face of Zut in the sea of faces below him.

He spotted the arch-traitor at last in the front line, flanked on one side by the obese Seti. Keeping one eye on the unholy pair he threw back his head, expanded his lungs and addressed himself to the multitude.

"Sons of Pthos," he began, "you have listened to evil words of council and have risen against your Queen. Know you that those who lead you, the evil Zut and the fat Seti, are willing to betray you unto death to achieve their own ends. . . .

"Queen Tamiris knows all. But the queen is merciful. Throw down your arms. Return you to your caves now and peace and justice shall reign again in Khalli."

He paused dramatically and a strained silence answered him. His commanding presence, his heavy, weighted words had made a deep impression on the blacks.

BEFORE the very walls of the City, with the power for which he had lusted so long, almost within his grasp, Zut saw that an overwhelming defeat confronted him. Worse yet, a defeat without having struck a blow.

A passionate hate for the jungle savage he had befriended welled up in his breast. But there was no time to consider that now. He had to act at once before the aroused slaves turned upon him and rent him limb from limb.

With a loud cry he leaped out from the rank and facing his followers raised his arms aloft. "Sons of Pthos!" he screamed. "Listen not to the words of the jungle savage. He has desecrated your temple and mocked your gods. The blood of the sacred leopard is upon his hands. Believe not that he is favored of Pthos. It was only by black magic that he shattered the idol of your protecting god."

His voice rose to a wild crescendo of passionate appeal. "Pthos cries out for vengeance! Kill the unbeliever, the profaner of your temple—kill those who harbor and shelter him. . . ."

A loud wail of approval and approbation went up from the slaves at the frenzied appeal. Spears were brandished, swords were thrust towards the walled city in a symbolic gesture.

And alone, immovable on top of the wall, looking down into a sea of hideous, lusting faces, Ka-Zar knew that he had lost. He flung up his arm again, holding the spear aloft. At the gesture the clamor subsided.

"So be it, sons of evil!" he bellowed. "You have asked for war and by war so shall ye die!"

His mighty torso arched suddenly backward. Balanced on one foot he poised for a moment. Then with a mighty thrust he hurled his spear from him. With an angry drone it sped true to its mark and the reckless black, who, in his eagerness for the taste of blood had leaped for the wall, was impaled in mid-stride.

The slave screamed once, dropped his weapons and with two clawing hands strove to tear the hardened bronze from his vitals. Then, with a final agonized wail he collapsed on his face.

Ka-Zar had drawn first blood. And in that second in which the dead slave had hit the hard packed earth, a hundred javelins were launched at his breast and a thousand men surged forward.

The siege of Khalli had begun.

CHAPTER XVIII

THE SIEGE

AND through seven long days and seven long nights the siege continued. Time and time again, like a black wave the slaves surged forward to the wall, only to be repulsed with frightful slaughter.

The ancient Egyptian builders of the lost city had done their work well. . . . The wall surrounding it was high, was thick. And so long as those defending it were faithful to their trust, almost impregnable.

Lashed on alike by fanatical zeal and blood lust the black slaves launched charge after charge against the frowning walls. While atop the parapet, the defenders hurled them back.

Full well they knew what fate awaited them if once the slaves succeeded in scaling the wall or breeching it. Outnumbered a hundred to one the white rulers of the city would be engulfed in a surging tide of black humanity. And the blood thirst of the ever insatiable Pthos would be slaked at last.

Of all those stout-hearted defenders, none showed more bravery, more daring, more reckless abandon than Ka-Zar. Wherever the fighting was hardest—wherever the walls were most sorely pressed, there would be found his herculean figure—there would be heard his defiant challenge of the lion.

Long since the attacking hordes had learned to fear it, to tremble before its might. And as the walls still held, in more than one heathen heart a doubt was born.

Ka-Zar fought with the strength and valor of ten men. He was untiring, ever vigilant—ever the first to jump into action when a new danger threatened.

Single-handed, alone, his companions swept to oblivion from about him, he fought off a score of raiding blacks until re-enforcements swept up beside him.

A dozen wounds scarred his mighty body. His eyes were red-rimmed and heavy from lack of sleep. Yet the arm that swung his mighty broad sword never failed him and his aim in hurling his long spears was never better.

Many times he longed for his stout bow and a full quiver of arrows. Bitterly he cursed himself for a fool for not having made one during his long idle days in Khalli. But moments of such futile contemplation were few and far between. It was hack with the broad sword! thrust with javelin!— and in close quarters fight for one's life with blood-stained dagger.

The first night of the siege he learned the purpose of the strange contraptions that had puzzled him. He saw men with straining backs, bend the stout saplings back like a bow; saw others load the small platform at their ends with heavy boulders.

Then, with a screaming rush of wind the saplings would be suddenly released and the heavy stone would hurtle over the wall to crash into the milling throng before the walls.

The contrivances were crude catapults but they were efficient and Ka-Zar marveled at them. A clean death and far to be preferred to the agony of boiling oil poured from the top of the parapet onto the heads of the blacks attempting to scale the wall.

Towards the close of the eighth day there came a temporary lull in the fighting. The decimated ranks of Zut's followers drew back from the wall out of spear range, leaving only a thin circle of warriors before the parapet to harry the defenders.

Grateful for the momentary respite Ka-Zar squatted on top of the wall and gave his attention to the knicked and dulled edge of his great sword. He was testing it with his thumb a few moments later, when Ankhamen limped hurriedly towards him.

The old man's face was drawn and pale but there was an indomitable light in his eyes. For a week he had been fighting gallantly at Ka-Zar's side, despite the fact that during the first night of the siege a spear had pierced his thigh.

Ka-Zar placed a bracing arm around the old man's shoulders. "The blacks retreat," he said cheerily. "They have tasted death and like it not."

Ankhamen smiled up at him and shook his head. "Would that it were so. It is but a respite. Zut has some new cunning afoot. His blacks but rest to gather strength for a new assault."

KA-ZAR frowned darkly and tested the blade of his sword again. "And how fares Tamiris, Queen of Khalli?"

For a fleeting second Ankhamen looked at him keenly, then turned away with a little sigh. "She is true daughter of the Pharaohs. Even in the face of ultimate defeat, her courage never falters."

At the words, Ka-Zar's head snapped up. "I understand you not, Ankhamen? Why speak of defeat when the blacks have fallen before us like flies? For seven days and seven nights they have stormed the walls and failed."

Ankhamen nodded. "If it were but a matter of defending the walls . . . But go. The Queen would talk with you."

"Tamiris?"

"Even so—Tamiris. She would look upon your face again, and she has words for your ear alone." He held out his hand in a simple gesture and instinctively Ka-Zar grasped it in his own. "Go," said Ankhamen again, "and may the gods that brought you here, preserve you. For the gods know that Khalli has need of you."

CHAPTER XIX

HUNGER

THE dark eyes of the Queen grew soft as she saw the lines of weariness etched in Ka-Zar's face, his care-worn brow, the still defiant angle of his lean jaw. She raised her hand in greeting as he approached and there was both anxiety and a melting tenderness in her voice as she asked: "How goes the siege, O brave Protector of Khalli?"

Ka-Zar shrugged his tired shoulders. "Your Egyptians are loyal and brave. All the legions of the devil cannot pass them."

Tamiris sighed. "No," she murmured huskily. "With such a leader, no one could admit defeat." Then lowering her eyes, she frowned, traced the pattern of the rug with the toe of a tiny gilded sandal. "But there is one enemy more powerful than even the mighty Ka-Zar. And now that enemy rears his ugly head here in the heart of Khalli."

Ka-Zar's eyes narrowed. "You mean . . .?"

"Hunger," answered Tamiris simply. "The supply of food is almost gone. Even the stoutest heart grows faint when the belly is empty."

Ka-Zar scowled. "There is food in the caverns of the blacks. There is game aplenty yet nearer at hand, in the forest." His hands clenched at his sides. "Yet your Egyptians are outnumbered, a hundred to one. To sally forth from the safety of the walls— means death."

Tamiris' eyes were haunted. She turned, walked unsteadily to the window and looked out over her beleaguered city. She raised a hand, brushed it across her ivory brow. "Must I, then," she asked faintly, "surrender? Turn my kingdom and my faithful subjects over to the mercies of these blood-crazed rebels?"

A hushed silence followed her words. Ka-Zar saw a swift vision of the slaughter, of the terrible fate of this unhappy girl, once the black horde poured in through the gates of the city. The prospect of a lingering death by starvation was equally unbearable.

He inhaled a sharp breath. His massive chest expanded; his nails dug into the palms of his clenched fists.

"No!" The word tore from his lips.

Tamiris whirled. Startled, she stared at him. And there was that determination written upon his face, that reckless glint in his eyes, that brought a faint ray of hope to her own.

She ran to him in a sudden burst of passion, placed her tiny hands upon his broad chest and turned her face up to his own.

"Speak!" she begged hoarsely. "There is yet hope?"

Ka-Zar seized her wrists, his fingers tightened about them until she winced with the pain.

"Ka-Zar will never surrender to the evil Zut!" he said, his face distorted, his amber eyes glinting fire. "Somehow—someway—he shall yet outwit him."

He thrust her roughly from him, turned and stalked across the room. With the lithe stride of Zar the lion he paced the width of the chamber, while Tamiris watched him, hardly daring to breathe. Suddenly he flung back his head, whirled to confront her.

"To send out an expedition for food would be fatal. This war must be ended swiftly—it is our only hope. Heed my words. These blacks who have dared to rise against you are but a pack of slinking jackals, brainless, without courage, helpless without a leader. Zut and Seti may be slain. Without those masters of evil to spur them on those jackals will flee yelping for their black holes."

Breathlessly Tamiris nodded. "True! You are keen as well as mighty, O Ka-Zar. But to slay Zut and Seti—how could that be done? I know those skulking schemers well. Surely they keep well away from the dangers of the battle. Doubtless they save their precious hides somewhere in the safety of the distant caverns."

Ka-Zar's lips curled with scorn. "So, too, thinks Ka-Zar. There he will go, there he will find them—and there his knife shall seek out and find their black hearts!"

THE fervor of his words brought a flush to Tamiris' cheeks. For a moment she exulted with him. Then suddenly she paled. One hand flew up to the ivory column of her throat.

"But—but Ka-Zar has said that not all the Egyptians together dare to venture from the walls. Who, then, goes with him to seek Zut and Seti?"

Slowly Ka-Zar drew himself up to the full of his majestic height. "Ka-Zar needs no companions," he said arrogantly. "They would but hinder him. He goes alone."

The last vestige of color drained from Tamiris' face. All her newborn hope turned to ashes in her mouth. She was torn between her last desperate chance for salvation and the love for this bronzed giant that filled her heart. Her slender body quivered from head to foot.

And while she stood as one turned to stone, unable to utter a sound, Ka-Zar turned abruptly and strode out of the room.

CHAPTER XX

THE POISON SPRING

WHEN he emerged from the palace, night had fallen over the lost kingdom and a misty glow on the horizon foretold the rising of the moon. Great stars studded the sky, remote, coldly indifferent to the woes of men on the insignificant earth so far beneath them. Like reflections of the stars on a dark lake, the camp-fires of the besiegers made a twinkling ring about the city.

Ka-Zar sent a messenger to Ankhamen, warning him only that he would be absent for a while and bidding him to stay on guard until he returned. Then anxious to run the gauntlet before the moon rose, he made his way swiftly down from terrace to terrace.

As always he was naked except for the skin of an animal about his loins, and save for the keen blade tucked into that belt, he was unarmed. He moved lithely as N'Jagi, as silently as Sinassa the snake. Even his own vigilant sentries did not see him as he slid like a shadow over the lowest rampart, dropped cat-like to the ground outside the walls.

His enemies, too, were weary of the prolonged warfare. They had retired to huddled groups about their fires, where they squatted and partook of their evening meal. But though the defenders of Khalli were silent in this brief respite, these slaves were already drunk with victory. Long before he reached their circle Ka-Zar could hear their voices raised in animated conversation, in discordant song, in quarrel among themselves.

He headed for a point where the blacks were encamped at the fringe of the encroaching jungle. From beyond the chatter about the camp fires there drifted the squeals of Quog the wild pig, the chattering of Nono's long-tailed brothers, the fiendish laugh of Janko the hyena. And as he listened to these familiar sounds, all the thin veneer of civilization that Ka-Zar had acquired from his contact with men, dropped from him. He became a beast once more—the two-legged, super-animal who was the lord of the jungle.

His massive shoulders dropped into a crouch. His eyes closed until they were but gleaming amber slits. His nostrils flared and he sniffed at the damp night air. As he glided forward his bronze body closely resembled the tawny form of his mighty brother.

It was amazing the way his huge form shrank to cover behind a stunted bush, disappeared behind the narrow bole of a tree. Gliding soundlessly from one patch of shadow to another he approached the nearest group of jabbering blacks.

They were ensconced beneath the spreading branches of a huge oulangi tree. Whether the firelight in their eyes blinded them, or whether their full bellies had lulled their caution, they lolled at their ease even as the black shadow of the jungle man rose from behind nearby shrubbery, flitted across an open stretch and melted into the huge bole of the tree. Ironically, one walked over, squatted down at its base and leaned his back against the rough bark.

Ka-Zar's lips pulled back from his teeth in a soundless snarl. His nostrils wrinkled from the strong, foetid odor of the unwashed black. It seemed incredible that the senses of these creatures could be so dulled that they had no warning of his presence.

One of his enemies yawned. Another scratched listlessly at the sole of his foot. One poked at the fire, sending a shower of sparks hissing up toward the branches. And still without the slightest sound, Ka-Zar swung himself upward, climbed hand over hand up the opposite side of the tree trunk.

Squatting on the lowest bough, he peered downward. What a keen pleasure it would be to drop, screeching, into the midst of these stupid Oman! Or to let the roar of the lion blast from his throat, causing them to scatter pellmell in all directions!

But the fate of a kingdom was at stake and this was no time to indulge in such heroics.

From the farthermost tip of the branch on which he squatted, there was but a short space to the dense forest growth beyond. Moving on his belly like a great snake, Ka-Zar worked his way out toward the end of the limb. There, clutching the branches, drawing his body back like an archer's bow, he let go. There was a breathless moment as he hurtled through empty air. Then his outstretched hands brushed foliage, caught a projecting tree branch and he swung up into a tall baobab.

HE kept to the trees. Like Chaka the ape he swung easily from branch to branch, traveling as swiftly as if he had been on the ground below. With a long, gliding swing he proceeded toward the heart of the jungle.

He paused at last in the dense foliage of a towering daboukra. Filling his lungs, spreading his brawny shoulders, he set the forest trembling with the stentorian roar of the lion.

A hush fell over the jungle, as in fear and terror, of that dreaded sound, all smaller animals scurried to cover. For a long moment the wilderness lay dark and silent under the slanting rays of the slender sickle moon, that rose above the rim of the cliffs. Ka-Zar cocked his head to one side and waited.

Then it came—drifting to him on the warm wind—the echoing rumble of Zar's answering call. Satisfied, Ka-Zar awaited the coming of his brother.

He had not long to wait. A faint breeze stirred the leaves, bringing with it a familiar, pungent scent. Then thirty paces away the undergrowth parted and a great tawny shape materialized on the forest floor.

With a low rumble of welcome in his throat, Ka-Zar dropped lightly down from his perch. Whining greetings were exchanged by these strange blood brothers.

"Trouble has come to these Oman," said Zar in guttural growls.

Ka-Zar nodded. "True, wise one," he answered. "But it shall soon be ended. Ka-Zar goes to slay the evil ones who have caused it. The fat black Om and the skinny white one, whose eyes are like those of Pindar the eagle. Nay," he corrected himself, "not Pindar—but Kru the vulture."

Golden gleams danced the depths of Zar's eyes. "No longer will Zar lie low in the forest," he said. "He goes with his brother."

Ka-Zar looked at his faithful friend and a burden lifted from his weary heart. When he had summoned the lion, he had hoped to hear those very words. So be it. Just they two—against enemies whose number was legion. No more of this Oman's warfare—they would fight like the jungle animals that they were.

There was no need to express his gratitude. He fingered the haft of the knife at his belt and said simply: "Come."

On soundless feet and padded paws, side by side, they traveled swiftly over the jungle floor toward the subterranean caverns under the cliffs. Their path paralleled the road that the people of Khalli had hewed through the forest. To their keen ears came the sound of much traffic across it now. Occasionally they caught glimpses of twinkling lights through the trees. Always fearful of the encroaching forest after nightfall, the blacks moved now in the safety of numbers and the light of flaring torches.

MAN and lion came at length to the last, dense clump of mangroves near the opening in the cliffs. There they crouched and waited, watching from slitted eyes for their opportunity to proceed further. Several times groups of slaves hurried past them, happily unaware of two pairs of glowing eyes that watched their movements from the nearby undergrowth. But in the jungle patience is as important as courage and not by the slightest sound did Ka-Zar or Zar betray their presence.

Their chance came at last. The open space between them and the cliffs was, for a brief interlude, empty of all but the gauzy light of the moon. Slipping from cover, they glided soundlessly across it, plunged abruptly into the darkness that brooded over the shores of the vast, subterranean lake.

As his most likely objective, Ka-Zar determined to go first to the Temple of Pthos. Zar voiced no question, fell obediently into place at his heels. Each time the glow of a torch illumined their path, they paused to make sure that no eyes were watching before they exposed themselves in the light. Several times they had to fall swiftly back into shadowy recesses, as parties of blacks came noisily along the muddy bank.

Without mishap they reached the spot where they must turn off to go to the temple. For some inexplicable reason Zar halted, hesitated. Ka-Zar frowned, looked questioningly at the lion. Then, as though drawn by some irresistible force, his eyes searched farther on. He froze in his tracks.

A figure emerged from a tunnel mouth some distance ahead. A sputtering flare was in its upraised hand and the flickering light illumined the obese form directly below it. There was no mistaking that monstrous, repellent creature. Ka-Zar's breath caught in his throat; Zar's lips curled back in a soundless snarl. It was Seti—the High Priest of Pthos.

Seti saw them at the same moment. His eyes bulged, his puffy cheeks turned an ashen gray. With a shrill wail of terror he clutched the torch tighter, turned and plunged back into the mouth of the tunnel.

Silently Ka-Zar and Zar bounded forward in hot pursuit. In a series of long leaps they gained the opening of the passage. Plunging in they raced after their quarry. They could hear his frightened yelps as he ran deeper and deeper into the bowels of the earth.

Ka-Zar's brain whirled. Though Seti's first scream had apparently raised no alarm, he realized that they must get the High Priest and silence him. For if the blacks once learned that he and Zar were in the heart of their stronghold, they would never escape. The slaves knew every twist and turning in this maze of passageways, but to Ka-Zar they were still strange, a menace and trap.

Though fear had lent wings to Seti's feet, his short stumpy legs were no match for theirs. They rounded a bend —slithered to a sudden halt. There before them stood Seti, at the edge of a bubbling pool. The torch was still clutched in his hand and his face was a mask of stark terror. When he saw the glittering knife in Ka-Zar's hand and the massive lion who crouched by Ka-Zar's side, his lips worked like soft rubber. A stream of saliva trickled from one corner of his mouth, then it opened and once more his paralyzed throat let a single shriek escape it.

HE turned to flee again, tripped over a stone, plunged headlong forward. The torch flew from his hand, struck the ground and shattered in a burst of spitting embers. In the ensuing darkness there came a mighty splash. Then the hairs at the back of Ka-Zar's neck bristled and in his ears rang the most awful cry he had ever heard—a mournful wail that rose to a high crescendo, died there in an ominous gurgle.

Sheathing his knife, he leaped forward, snatched up the fallen torch, blew upon its smouldering tip. It burst into flame again and holding it high, he stepped toward the pool.

The waters slapped and frothed against the sides. With his free hand outstretched, Ka-Zar waited for Seti's head to bob up again. Behind him, Zar whined.

But gradually the tossing waters subsided—and the High Priest failed to reappear. Ka-Zar was silent. There was awe in his heart as he knelt by the pool. For some reason he felt no exultation that one of his hated enemies had met his death.

He became aware of a faint, acrid odor. He wrinkled his nostrils. He sniffed, raised his eyes about him. Then he lowered his head a trifle more over the bubbling pool.

The unpleasant odor was stronger— it emanated from the water. A vague thought, that eluded him, disturbed Ka-Zar's brain. He dipped a little of the water up in his palm, touched his tongue to the liquid.

It burned like fire at the contact. With a gesture of revulsion he spilled the water from his hand, wiped his palm on his belt. He was very sober as he rose to his feet, turned silently to the crouching lion. For that vague thought had crystallized in his brain—he knew now that this was the poison spring— these were the terrible waters of the Cup of Pthos.

It took much to shake the stout heart of Ka-Zar, king of the jungle. But his step was a trifle unsteady as he led Zar back down the tunnel through which they had come.

CHAPTER XXI

THE SECRET TUNNEL

BUT an enemy is an enemy. And an enemy dead is not a matter to brood about, but to forget. By the time they emerged once more on the bank of the lake, Ka-Zar's step was again springy and his mind busy with other matters.

Seti was disposed of. There yet remained Zut, the more important of that ungodly pair. Again Ka-Zar headed for the Temple of Pthos in search of the counselor.

Now that he had cast aside the customs of men and become an animal again, Fortune once more smiled upon him. He and Zar met no one as they strode down the long passageway, came at last to the bronze door of the temple. Thrusting it cautiously inward, Ka-Zar peered first into the great dim chamber beyond. Only the low snarl of the chained leopard greeted him. With a low growl to Zar to follow, he stepped inside, let the lion enter and then shut the massive portal behind him.

At the sight of the crouching black form near the wall, the long hairs on the back of the lion's neck rose to a stiff ruff. The tuft at the tip of his tail switched. His lips pulled back from his fangs. Confronted now by two such formidable enemies, N'Jagi quivered down his supple length. His fear was greater than his hate as he spat. But Ka-Zar was not concerned with the old feud between them, right now. He dropped a hand on Zar's head and the low growl that rumbled in the lion's throat subsided.

Turning their backs on the captive beast, they surveyed the dim reaches of the temple. Ka-Zar saw with keen disappointment that except for the presence of the leopard, they were alone. The remains of the idol still lay where they had fallen on the night when he had toppled the grinning image from its throne. It was highly probable that during the bloody war that had broken out immediately after, no one had even entered the temple.

Zar moved forward, sniffing. Cautiously he climbed up the dais, nosed curiously about in the wreckage. Ka-Zar turned, wondering where next to seek for Zut. The death of Seti accomplished nothing unless he sent the scheming counsellor to join his fat-faced accomplice.

He had almost reached the door when a low whine from Zar spun him around. He looked up to see Zar sinking from sight!

He bounded forward but even as he leaped up the steps of the dais, Zar leaped back to safety. Together they stared down at something so unbelievable that for a moment both doubted the evidence of their eyes.

On the very spot where the base of the huge idol had stood, a square block of stone had tilted downward. Cautiously Ka-Zar stooped, found that it took all his strength to thrust it back yet further. It was a cleverly-concealed trap-door and judging from the way its rusted hinges squeaked, it had been many, many years since it had last been opened.

At first he wondered vaguely why, when Zut had concealed himself in the idol, he had not fallen through. Then he realized that it had been the tremendous weight of the lion that had caused the trap to drop. Quite possibly—he did not know that he guessed the truth —even the all-knowing Zut had never suspected its existence.

Together he and Zar peered down

the opening. In the dim light all they could make out was a flight of cut stone steps leading down into the blackness.

With a thoughtful frown wrinkling his brow, Ka-Zar squatted at the edge of the aperture and considered. Though their presence in the underground caverns was not yet suspected, there was still a good chance that they would be caught before they could get out of the catacombs. He had to find Zut—true. But he did not have the faintest idea where to look for him and somehow, this gaping hole had a growing fascination for him.

He looked at Zar, voiced his indecision in a low whine.

Calmly Zar answered. "Zar goes where his brother goes."

KA-ZAR waited for no more. Dropping lithely over the edge of the hole, he landed on the stone steps. Zar followed.

There was a bronze ring on the under side of the slab. Lest the secret trap door be discovered while they were below, Ka-Zar closed it behind them. He braced his legs on the steps, but it took all his mighty strength to raise the block of stone to the level of the platform above.

With the closing of the aperture, they were left in utter blackness. Feeling their way cautiously they descended the flight of steps. Down—down—down. . . .

Then abruptly they struck a level earth floor. Feeling about with his outstretched hands, Ka-Zar found that they stood in a narrow, low tunnel. He hesitated but a moment. It made small difference whether they turned right or left. At random, he chose the left.

The passage was very narrow and so low that he had to stoop well over as he moved cautiously forward. Even his jungle-trained eyes could not see his hand before him in the abysmal blackness. If any crawling dangers lurked in the tunnel, he and Zar would be struck before they sensed their peril.

But nothing stirred or moved. Here not even the drip of water broke the profound stillness. Apparently all living creatures shunned these lowest depths.

The passage twisted and turned like a snake, straightened out again, then at last began a gradual ascent. Were Ka-Zar's eyes deceiving him? Or was the blackness a shade lighter?

A few moments later he knew that he was right. The Stygian gloom gave way gradually to a dim twilight, which in turn brightened with every step. And at last up ahead was light—a diffused bluish radiance that could only be the effulgence of the moon!

They broke into a run, came to an abrupt halt at the end of the tunnel. They were standing at the bottom of a sheer shaft. But unlike the precipitous hole down which they had first tumbled from the upper earth, this shaft was scalable! Steps had been cut into the rock walls—a long flight of stairs that wound round and round clear up to the level of the world above.

Here was the end of Ka-Zar's long search for an outlet from the lost kingdom! By sheer accident Zar had discovered a long-forgotten, secret exit. The way to freedom—the way back to their dearly-beloved jungle—was clear before them.

With a single, joyous leap Zar gained the fifth step, looked back eagerly for Ka-Zar to follow. But the bronzed giant did not move.

With an impatient growl, Zar urged him to come. To his bewilderment, Ka-Zar sadly shook his head.

"No." The single guttural syllable rumbled in his throat. "Go back to the forest, O mighty Zar. Your faithful mate, your stalwart sons, your jungle people wait anxiously for your coming.

Ka-Zar will follow. But first there is work to be done. Ka-Zar has given his word and Ka-Zar must not break faith."

Zar crouched on the step, whined.

"Go," repeated Ka-Zar. "Soon Ka-Zar will be free to follow. He will find Nono also—we must not desert the silly one."

Zar whined again. His eyes turned up longingly toward the patch of midnight sky far above.

With heavy heart Ka-Zar raised a bronzed arm in farewell salute, then turned abruptly on his heel.

But before he had taken three strides back into the dim tunnel, the massive form of Zar fell silently into place again at his heels.

Ka-Zar's heart was choked by an emotion that could not be expressed in words. With a low cry he dropped to his knees beside the great lion, clenched his hands in the shaggy mane and laid his cheek against the tawny fur. Then with a lighter heart, he sprang once more to his feet and started back at a long, swinging stride.

HE did not stop until they stood once more under the trap-door that opened into the Temple of Pthos. Before them the mysterious tunnel went yet farther.

Ka-Zar leaned over and spoke gutturally into the ear of the lion. "To go back as we have come is dangerous. Many Oman stir in the caves. Already we have found the way out of this evil place. Shall Ka-Zar go now in the other direction, to see what lies there?"

Zar's answer was simple and given without a second's hesitation—a single growl of assent.

And so the two set forth down the tunnel. As before, the passageway wound and twisted, turned back on itself, veered off again at a tangent. Even the keen sense of direction that was a heritage of these jungle creatures failed them. There was neither moon nor star nor breath of air to tell them where they went, only blackness hemmed in on both sides by walls of rock.

This time they traveled longer than it had taken them to find the shaft at the opposite end. They traveled until Zar's paws grew tender from the rough floor, until Ka-Zar began to wonder whether the passage was truly endless.

Always, though, they maintained their caution. Zar felt his foothold at every step, lest a pitfall send him hurtling downward. Ka-Zar kept one hand on the wall at his side, the other thrust out before him.

Then abruptly the floor of the tunnel sloped steeply upward—up, up, a hundred paces until Ka-Zar was halted by a blank wall.

Groping about him in the impenetrable gloom, he discovered a trap-door, like the one that opened into the temple, directly above his head. The roof of the passage here was very low and without difficulty he located the metal ring in its center.

He growled softly to Zar. "Here is another entrance made long ago by the Oman. Whither it leads, Ka-Zar does not know. What waits on the other side—danger—death—a trap—Ka-Zar cannot tell. But he shall soon know!"

Zar's only answer was to crouch back on his powerful haunches. They would leap out together—face whatever fate awaited them on the far side of that block of stone.

Ka-Zar grasped the bronze ring with both hands, gritted his teeth and with all the strength at his command, pulled it downward. The slab yielded slowly at first, its rusty hinges protesting. Then as Ka-Zar heaved again, it dropped, disclosing a square aperture.

With an agile spring, his hand ready at the hilt of his knife, he leaped through the opening. Fangs bared, ears flattened back against his skull, Zar vaulted up beside him.

For a moment both stared blankly about them, blinking their eyes in the light of the moon after their long hours in the absolute darkness below. Nothing moved or stirred. Then suddenly Ka-Zar flung back his head and laughed.

He recognized this place—it was a little-used blind alley that ran directly back of Tamiris' palace.

CHAPTER XXII

Plan of Campaign

LEAVING Zar to wait for him, Ka-Zar sped swiftly through the deserted halls of the palace on his way to the Queen's apartments.

For the second time that night he pushed through the heavy door without the formality of announcing his coming. On his entrance, Tamiris whirled from the balcony, where she had been brooding over her beleaguered city.

Then with a little, glad cry she recognized the bronzed figure in the doorway and with hands outstretched she ran to meet him.

Without thinking, Ka-Zar clasped her tiny hands in his own, looked deep into her melting eyes. The Queen veiled hers at last with long lashes and a little breathlessly she drew away.

"Ka-Zar!" she breathed with a long-drawn sigh of relief. "Merciful Isis has heard my prayer and has answered it. You return safely once more to Khalli. You have succeeded?"

"By half," said Ka-Zar. "The fat-bellied Seti is dead—a victim to his own well of poison—to the bitter waters of his own god."

Tamiris' eyes lit up with exultation, then clouded over. "And Zut—you found him not?"

Ka-Zar shook his head. "No. But Ka-Zar had discovered something else. Ka-Zar has a plan that may yet defeat the hordes of blacks and save your city, O Tamiris."

"Speak," she said urgently. "My life—nay, that means nothing—my kingdom is in your hands."

Swiftly Ka-Zar told her of the secret tunnel he had stumbled on; how it led from the very wall of the palace beneath them to the spot in the Temple of Pthos where the fallen idol had stood.

"From the state of this passage," continued Ka-Zar, "no man knows of its existence. Not even the all-knowing Zut, for many, many moons have passed since it has last been used."

"And your plan?" continued Tamiris eagerly, impatient for him to continue.

"A simple one," answered Ka-Zar. "At the head of a hundred of your picked men, Ka-Zar will lead the way through the tunnel. Then while Ankhamen makes a great show of fight from the walls of the city, we will fall upon Zut and his warriors from the rear in a surprise attack.

"In the instant we strike, Ankhamen is to throw open the gate and sally forth with his men. Thus, caught between our two forces, Zut's slaves will be dazed and will fall easy victim to our spears and swords." He drew himself up to his full height. "Ka-Zar will see that Zut escapes him not a second time."

Tamiris' eyes were bright with a new hope—and with something else, too—when he had finished.

"Well conceived, O mighty Ka-Zar," she exclaimed. "It shall be done as you say. The pick of my men shall follow you." With an eager step she crossed the room to a gilded cord that hung by her bed. She jerked it twice and somewhere deep in the palace a brazen gong clanged. Then she returned and stood by Ka-Zar's side. All her old arrogance had deserted her. With bowed head she stood before him, humble, meek.

"True, I have prayed to the goddess Isis that Khalli might be saved," she murmured. "But I have prayed more you be spared the evil fortunes of war. Oh Ka-Zar. . . ."

But Ka-Zar was not to know then the confession that was in her heart. A heavy fist sounded on the portal. At a word from Tamiris the door opened and Ankhamen strode into the room. For a moment he stared with open-eyed amazement at Ka-Zar, then made a low obeisance before the Queen.

"Rise, faithful Ankhamen," said Tamiris. "And behold in Ka-Zar the saviour of Khalli. He has a plan conceived by the gods. And something in my heart tells me that it will not fail."

CHAPTER XXIII

The Battle and What Followed

AN hour later, Ka-Zar and Zar once more descended down the sheer black slope of the tunnel. But this time they were not alone. In single file a hundred soldiers followed them. Flares lighted the way but though they were deep in the bowels of the earth, Ka-Zar took no further chances. Silence was the strict order. And the tunnel stirred only to the shuffle of many feet and the occasional clink of metal.

When they emerged from the dim temple, Fortune still favored the jungle god. There were no warriors to be seen and only a few hags, terrified at the sight of Ka-Zar, the mighty lion and the file of armed men, scurried for their holes and stayed quaking in them.

And so by what seemed a miracle they made their way through the jungle and came at last within sight of their enemies, without a single alarm having been raised.

For a long hour, tense, alert, every sense and perception on trigger edge, Ka-Zar crouched low in the dense tangle of forest that encroached on the clearing surrounding the beleaguered ramparts of Khalli. Resting on the ground before him was a ponderous, two-bladed sword. By his s i d e crouched the faithful Zar, the hairs of his mane standing stiff and erect. Behind his back, already over their first fear of the great beast, lay a hundred of Tamiris' most trusted warriors.

They had been hand-picked by Ankhamen himself. And before following Ka-Zar into the secret tunnel, each man had sworn that for him there would be no retreat that night.

Now they waited, impatient, eager for the final conflict while the moon slipped slowly down the western sky.

Before them, in the open clearing before the city, Zut's men still stormed about the walls. With each long day of the fruitless seige their blood lust had increased. They were a mob, a pack of hungry wolves closing in for the kill.

The sweat of impatience standing out on his brow, even though the air was chill, Ka-Zar watched as the pale moon dipped at last behind the surrounding cliffs. An instant later, as if unseen hands were pulling it, a carpet of dark shadow raced out from the walls and engulfed his hiding place and his men.

With a long, pent-up sigh of relief he snatched up his sword and rose swiftly to his feet. As one, the men behind him rose with him. Zar was already bellying forward to the edge of the jungle wall.

With the jungle giant in the lead, the raiding party edged cautiously forward a few feet until they stood on the very edge of the clearing. There was grim resolution in every man's eye as he silently picked out his first victim. Muscles bulged, bellies tautened.

Ka-Zar turned to his men and issued his last order. "At the call of the lion, break a long pace from the jungle into the open—let go your spears in a single volley—then close with swinging sword."

The men nodded. Ka-Zar turned back once more to the clearing, saw that Zar's mighty back was already arched for the spring. His tawny eyes became flecked with steel. A great joy was in his heart. First he would save the Queen and her lost city, then with Zar at his side and Nono on his shoulder, he would traverse for the last time the underground passageways—to freedom. To freedom and his jungle domain.

With a sudden exultant movement he flung back his head. His chest expanded to the full and the rumbling roar of the lion crashed from his lips. With the cry still rattling in his throat he leaped forward. Behind him, with the hoarse shouting of a thousand men instead of a meager hundred, his men followed after him.

A SHRILL wail of alarm went up from the slaves at the sudden, unexpected onslaught. And as they turned to face the new danger that threatened them, the air became suddenly alive with hungry, steel-tipped spears.

Not a spear was wasted. Every one found its mark. The charge of the slaves was checked in confusions. And as the blacks recoiled before the slashing advance of Ka-Zar and his men, Ankhamen threw open the gate of the City and at the head of his men sallied forth.

The maneuver was executed with neatness and dispatch. Caught between two lines of charging steel the slaves were thrown into a panic. The only explanation they had for this sudden attack on their rear was that Pthos, their god of darkness, had deserted them—that Isis had prevailed.

And then over the din and clatter of battle, Ka-Zar heard the voice of Zut. The counsellor had earlier, during the lull in the fighting when Ka-Zar had made his secret sally out of Khalli, gone from the caves to the battle-front. He had come only to exhort his black horde to victory, planning a thundering assault on the city on the morrow. Now he had been trapped with his men and his shrill voice rose in a frantic effort to lash them on.

In vain.

Even the will of their leader could not help them now.

Ka-Zar's pulses leaped as he finally made out the gaunt form of his enemy, striking out blindly at friend and foe alike in a sudden panic as he realized that defeat was inevitable. He plunged heedlessly in that direction, his great sword flashing death to right and left, with Zar dealing terror beside him.

But many men were between Ka-Zar and the man he wanted so desperately to reach. Zut saw him coming from a distance, saw the huge lion that sent the blacks shrieking in all directions. The blood turned to water in Zut's veins. His craven heart almost stopped beating. Then in mad panic he burst through the ranks of the slaves and with his tattered robes whipping about his skinny legs, plunged headlong into the forest and headed toward the distant caves.

Ka-Zar saw him disappear—voiced his fury, not in the language of Khalli but in a guttural snarl to Zar.

Together they redoubled their savage onslaught, working their way toward the point where Zut had vanished. Their path was a bloody one. Blacks screamed and died before Ka-Zar's flashing sword; met a fearful fate before the sabre claws and dripping fangs of the mighty Zar. It was the presence of the massive lion, as much as anything else, that accounted for the rout.

They were free of the milling press at last. With low growls rumbling in their throats, the mighty brothers of the jungle plunged into the underbrush that fringed the forest. Ka-Zar took to the trees, swinging in long flights from bough to bough to keep pace with the charging lion below. He had a keen intuition that Zut was fleeing to but one place—the Temple of Pthos. It seemed fitting and proper, fore-ordained that the denouement between them should take place in that dim vaulted chamber, amid the ruins of the image of the god.

Whether the hate in his heart had sharpened his senses, or whether it was merely the suggestion of his own mind, Ka-Zar thought he could still catch the hated scent of Zut on the sultry air. But the fleeing counsellor had had a fair start and mortal fear had lent wings to his feet.

They caught no sight of him as they burst from the jungle, raced to the opening in the cliffs and headed up the shore of the lake. But when they turned at last into the tunnel that led to the temple, there was no doubt about the scent that assailed their nostrils. A powerful odor is given off by beast—or man— in the grip of mortal fear. Both jungleman and lion caught the scent, realized its significance. Already the taste of victory was theirs and they made the passage reverberate to their roars.

THE bronze door of the temple was closed but with a reckless courage, Ka-Zar flung it open and the pair bounded across the threshold.

Just inside the portal they slid to a sudden halt.

On the opposite side of the vast chamber stood Zut, his face ashen-gray and his eyes haggard. Crouched at his feet was N'Jagi and Zut's hand was on the leopard's chain.

Ka-Zar's intuition had led him to the right place.

The hand of the treacherous counsellor had never known weapons. He flinched now at the sight of Ka-Zar's blood-stained sword. In his mad panic he had come to the one friend he had in Khalli—the one creature who would lay down his life to defend him.

Leopard and lion faced each other across the dim stretch that separated them. Then the shrill scream of N'Jagi and the challenging roar or Zar blended in a blast that made the very walls tremble. Ka-Zar dropped a hand to his friend's neck, restrained him.

"A fitting combat," he shouted to Zut. "Ka-Zar against Zut—my brother against yours. A kingdom for the victors! Death for the vanquished! Loose the leopard, O Zut!"

Already the ring of triumph was in his voice. Zut heard it and his bloodless lips could not answer. Instead, he fumbled with the chain, snapped open the glittering link that joined N'Jagi's collar. He pointed a trembling, bony finger at the bronzed giant and the tawny lion in the doorway. A thin trickle of saliva drooled from the corner of his mouth as he urged the beast forward.

"Slay them!" he mumbled. "For long years Zut has fed and nursed you. Now defend your master!"

N'Jagi's ears flattened against his skull. His lips pulled back from his teeth and his emerald eyes glared malevolently. With a single lithe bound he sprang to the middle of the temple, stopped in a crouch.

Near the portal Zar and Ka-Zar tensed. For a moment not a sound broke the stillness but their hoarse breathing. N'Jagi snarled—a low, strangled sound that started deep down in his throat. He glared at the pair in the doorway. And fear crept into his glittering orbs.

Once before he had fought with the two-legged one—had been at the point of death. Now beside him stood N'Jagi's hereditary enemy—the most enormous lion he had ever seen! For a moment the devils of hate battled with the fear in N'Jagi's black heart. Then suddenly he realized that his enemies stood between him and the door. The vague notion that he was trapped was too much for him. An eerie whine came from his throat.

Zut, too, was in the grip of a terrible fear. In a sudden desperation he stepped forward, cried out to N'Jagi: "Fall upon them! Rend them with your claws! Tear them with your fangs!"

The hairs along the leopard's spine quivered. The tip of his tail lashed back and forth. With a hunted look in his green eyes he glanced first at Ka-Zar and the lion, then at the frightened man who egged him on.

Suddenly a red film dimmed his eyes. The fact that Zut was his master was wiped from his animal brain. Zut's shrill voice was hateful in his ears. A blind fury, such as he had never known, filled his heart. With a hideous scream he gathered his haunches under him and sprang—sprang straight at his paralyzed master!

TOO late Zut flung up his hands in horror. Too late he stumbled backward. The black fury was upon him— ripping, clawing, snarling. And this time the scream of the leopard blended with another sound—a quavering cry of mortal anguish. Claws of pointed steel dug deep into Zut's vitals; N'Jagi's

foetid breath was hot on his face as he crashed to the ground.

For a moment Ka-Zar forgot their own hatred of these two, as they stared at the bloody spectacle. The smell, the taste of blood sent N'Jagi berserk. He clawed the lifeless body of his protector until nothing remained but a torn thing of mangled flesh and tattered rags.

Then suddenly his flat black head came up and he spat in the direction of the doorway. His fear was gone, now. It was not courage, either, but sheer madness that made him spring across the temple.

With a rumbling growl, Zar bounded out from under Ka-Zar's hand. Like a tawny fury he met the leopard's charge with one of his own.

And Ka-Zar, clutching his knife, stayed his own hand to watch the most magnificent spectacle of the jungle— Zar, aroused, terrible in all his might.

Leopard and lion met in mid-air and the crushing shock of the impact sent them both sprawling. But neither loosed his hold and they rolled over and over, slashing, clawing, ripping.

N'Jagi fought for his life. And Zar —to hold the supremacy with which he reigned over all the beasts of the wilderness. The lion was heavier, but the lithe black leopard was faster.

Breathing fast, his nostrils flared, his tawny eyes gleaming, Ka-Zar watched the death struggle between the two great beasts. He could not have taken a hand if he wished, for it was almost impossible to distinguish friend from foe in that whirling mass of black and tawny fur. He knew, also, that Zar would hold it a deadly insult if he interfered.

Back and forth they battled across the width of the temple. And now a trail of crimson spattered their wake.

Then suddenly a piercing screech echoed in the vaulted chamber. It died abruptly. A massive tawny body rose. Ka-Zar could see Zar's jaws still clamped about the throat of his enemy. The great lion shook the limp black body beneath him from side to side. Then his jaws relaxed their grip and the leopard lay still—never to move again.

Slowly, majestically, Zar turned to face his brother in the doorway. His regal head came up and it seemed strangely fitting that the Temple of Pthos, with the shattered idol of its god, with the body of its unholy guardian lifeless on the floor, should echo to the defiant rumble of the jungle lord's kill.

CHAPTER XXIV

Freedom

BY the time Ka-Zar and Zar reached the battle-ground, the fighting was over. A few victorious warriors still harassed groups of fleeing blacks, but most of the slaves had long since fled into the wilderness or scurried into caverns in the cliffs.

The triumphant Egyptians lined the ramparts of the tiered city, clustered about the gates that were now thrown wide. They greeted the appearance of Ka-Zar and the lion with a concerted cheer that made the valley ring.

The stately figure of Ankhamen moved up as they neared the gate.

"You have done your part well," Ka-Zar told him. "You have struck straight and true and Ka-Zar is proud to call you comrade."

Ankhamen bowed low. "I could ask for no greater reward than the words my leader has just spoken," he answered gravely. "Fain would I sing your praises, O mighty Ka-Zar. But I must not delay you. The Queen anxiously awaits your coming in the palace."

It was a procession of state that escorted Ka-Zar and the great lion up through the city. All the way was lined with the inhabitants of Khalli, who had thronged out to see their bronzed god. Ka-Zar could not restrain the ghost of a bitter smile as he remembered that he had first entered the city in chains. By his side Zar padded majestically along, proudly aloof to the cheers of these Oman whom he would always despise.

Their escort left them at the gates of the palace. There were pleased smiles and sly winks exchanged behind their backs as alone the pair made their way to the apartments of the Queen.

Again Tamiris had decked herself out in all her most resplendent raiment. This time she was sheathed in white like an alabaster statue, glittering with gems and swirling feathers. The breath caught in Ka-Zar's throat as he entered the room and she rose to meet him.

She took one step forward—then stopped. She stiffened as she saw the great tawny lion who stood at Ka-Zar's side.

It was a tribute to her courageous heart that she neither moved nor cried out at the sight of Zar, for this was the first time that she had ever been near such a terrifying beast.

"Fear not my brother," cried Ka-Zar, stepping to meet her. "Fear nothing again. Zut is dead—slain by his own hideous guardian of the Temple of Pthos. Ka-Zar has given you back your throne."

Tamiris stretched out her hands. Her cheeks were flushed, her eyes starry. "And Tamiris lays it at your feet, O mighty lord of the jungle," she said huskily. "All my pride has crumbled to ashes. I see that in your eyes that I have longed to see there—and that is enough. You do not speak—so I do it for you. Come to me, Ka-Zar!"

She let her hands drop to her sides, palms turned forward. It was an eloquent gesture. Her regal head tilted back, her scarlet lips parted, her firm breast high, she offered herself to him.

Ka-Zar felt strangely awed, humbled. He had a mad impulse to fling himself before her, bury his hot face in the folds of her snowy draperies, kiss her tiny sandaled feet.

Surely no ordinary mortal would have hesitated. But then, Ka-Zar was no ordinary mortal.

WITH a courtly gesture that he had never been taught, he dropped to one knee and bowed his head.

"Gracious Queen," he said mournfully, "Ka-Zar could find no greater happiness than to stay forever by your side. But his heart is heavy within him. There is a duty that calls."

A spasm of pain crossed Tamiris' face. Her cheeks paled, but slowly she nodded. She was a daughter of the Ptolemies and she knew the stern demand of duty.

Ka-Zar looked appealingly up at her. "The kingdom of Tamiris is once more safe," he explained. "But how fares Ka-Zar's jungle domain? He must return there to see, to make sure that peace and quiet reign over the wilderness." He rose to his feet, took her tiny hands in his own and looked into her eyes with such burning depths in his own that she quivered under his stare. "But Ka-Zar shall return," he said simply.

Once more Ka-Zar, with Nono atop his shoulder and Zar beside him, stood at the base of the steep shaft that led from the secret tunnel to the world above. And this time, as Zar bounded joyfully up the steps hewn in the rocky walls, his brother followed eagerly in his wake.

With exultant hearts they emerged, stood for a moment to drink in the precious draught of freedom. The immense blue bowl of the sky was high and cloudless above them. A dim speck in the azure vastness, Kru the vulture sailed on motionless pinions. A vagrant breeze stirred the long locks of Ka-Zar's hair, brought to his nostrils mingled odors of the distant places through which it traveled—the perfume of flowers, the rushes that edged a lake, the damp scent of the jungle. He inhaled deeply, filled his mighty lungs.

Nono chattered with delight. Zar raised his massive head and gave vent to a joyous roar.

They had come out on the side of a bare, rock-strewn bank. Above them the earth rose sheer toward the top of the tumbled, inaccessible cliffs that hemmed in the lost valley. Zar swung his head slowly from side to side, his amber eyes narrowed. Then with a leap, he bounded up the face of the bank.

His hind leg dislodged a heavy stone. It tore loose from its moorings, rolled over and over with swiftly-increasing momentum. Earth and pebbles followed it in a sliding rush—that increased in volume with every yard.

Ka-Zar whirled, cried out. Zar's legs were already going out from under him. He struggled to escape the landslide that he had created, dug in deep with his claws as with an ominous rumble the whole face of the bank came crashing downward.

Ka-Zar gained safety with a series of mighty leaps. Zar slid for some distance on the crest of the landslide, then with a last desperate effort, managed to bound clear of the falling earth.

The air was suddenly obscured by fine particles of heavy dust. The trio choked, coughed as the stuff got into their nostrils.

At last it gradually subsided and the air cleared again. And as it did, a low cry of dismay broke from Ka-Zar's lips.

The shaft from which they had just come—the opening to the secret tunnel—was no longer visible! With a whine he leaped back to the place where he had stood a few moments before, pawed wildly at the earth. But to no avail. The secret entrance and exit of the lost kingdom was sealed—closed forever!

THE vision of the Queen Tamiris, as he had last seen her, rose up before Ka-Zar's eyes. With the keenest anguish he realized that never would he see her again. Bravely she would wait for him to return. And then when at last she learned about the sealing of the tunnel, she would go back to her lonely throne.

With haunted eyes he turned to look at Zar. And the lion instinctively averted his head.

Swift, keen suspicion flashed to Ka-Zar's brain. Zar had not been able to understand the words that he and Tamiris had exchanged at their parting. But the wise lion's eyes were keen—he would have read their words in their eloquent eyes.

Had Zar done this on purpose? Had Zar started this landslide—risking his own life—so that his brother would not leave the jungle to return to Khalli? A terrible rage flared in Ka-Zar's breast.

He knew that he had guessed the truth.

Then slowly his wrath died within him. Perhaps, after all, Zar was right. The wilderness was his home. Quite probably the frail hands of a woman— even such a glorious creature as Tamiris—would fail to hold him in the confines of the sunken valley.

His shoulders squared. The sun gleamed on his bronzed body as he drew himself erect. The gentle fingers of the breeze touched his cheek, played with his hair. With a precious memory, but no sorrow in his heart he turned toward the direction of his jungle home and with a single guttural growl to Zar, said: "Come."

Freedom was his—freedom not only of body but of spirit—as with a glad rumble deep in his throat, Zar fell into place at his side and the trio headed for home.

THE END

Baseball is in again!

—and you'll be wanting your sports magazines crammed with home runs and southpaw pitchers . . . yes, and you can get it in a Red Circle sports magazine! In the latest issue of COMPLETE SPORTS you'll find FOUR baseball yarns, three of them novelettes!

(1) THE TROUBLEMAKER by Jonsey Taylor

(2) THE TANGO KID by Ross Kenton

(3) SMOKE BALL! by Arthur Mann

(4) PITCH WITH YOUR BRAINS by Charlie Lewis

And that's only part of the program in this swell, big issue! We give you SEVEN more action-packed short stories! . . . about your favorite sports too:—Boxing, Football, Auto Racing, Track, Tennis, Horse Racing, and Fight. TAKE THE TIP AND GET YOUR COPY NOW!

COMPLETE SPORTS is one of the three Red Circle sports magazines. Look for the Red Circle on the cover!

Assassin's Blood

by W. M. F. Bayliss

Busted out of the service and seeking nothing but revenge,
Hicks gets a chance to prove he's a real man—the hard way.

EX-CONVICT BILL HICKS squatted native fashion on the steps of Lahore mosque. His toes, sticking out at the ends of his seedy boots, were white with dust, the brim of his ancient straw hat flapped in the warm breeze. Under his stubby red beard, his face was grim.

"Damn him," he muttered, "wonder where he is now."

His big hands opened and shut convulsively and his blue eyes gleamed with a fierce light. He was thinking, not for the first time of the young Mohammedan clerk who had framed him with all the subtle cunning of a master. The man had got away with the bank's money and was still somewhere in India, rich and honored, while he, Bill Hicks—

Iron clattered on the stones below and he looked down. A lean man in khaki was pushing a big horse through the throng. He started and sprang to his feet. Colonel Ruddock! What was he doing here, far away from his rambling old bungalow in its rose garden beyond the city? Smiling, he hurried forward, but the Colonel did not draw rein, or show any sign of recognition. Only as he passed, his eyes glanced down meaningly, and then turned back to his long raw-hide whip, against which three fingers made an almost imperceptible movement. Bill looked after him in surprise. Something was afoot, something urgent and secret. He thought for a moment. Rawhide. Three fingers. Simple enough. A rendezvous at the skinner's bazaar, that stinking place outside the city limits at three o'clock. Pretty quick off the mark, the Colonel, but why this mystery all of a sudden? He smiled bitterly. Maybe it wasn't so strange after all. Even the Colonel might think twice about talking to a scarecrow in public. Yes, that must be the answer. He settled down again thoughtfully.

The many-colored crowd ebbed around the steps, farmers, beggars, merchants, all the types of the Punjab, but Bill did not see them. He was looking back into the past, thinking of someone he had known long ago, Bill Hicks, the smart young bank teller. A smile played for a moment among the untidy red bristles on his cheeks. Those were good days, but they did not last. After them came another man, older, grimmer, chafing behind bars against fate and his own folly.

Well, he had learned something during that dark time, thanks to one man. Queer how Colonel Ruddock had never lost interest in him, always bringing him books, talking with him, showing him strange angles of the invisible Eastern world outside the prison gates. It had almost looked as though the Colonel believed in him, even though he never said so. Bill sighed. Thanks to that one friend the nightmare had passed. This easy life was not so bad when you got used to it although sometimes—

The muffled thunder of a gun set the pigeons wheeling around the great blue dome behind him and Bill rose to his feet. It was noon. He must go to meet the Colonel.

The skinners' bazaar was a group of sheds far out on a white hot plain, above which a cloud of vultures wheeled, waiting for carcasses. A blind man could find his way there, thought Bill miserably as he puffed the stench from his nostrils and hurried forward. A doubt assailed him. Could he have got the message wrong, by any chance? No white man ever came here, and both he and the Colonel would show up like lighthouses. Strange, very strange.

Suddenly he came to the bank of a ravine, one of those sudden deep clefts which appear without warning, dry now, but raging torrents in the rains. Something among the shadows at the bottom moved, and there was a dull plop, like the drawing of a cork. Bill peered downward.

"Come here," called an English voice, and he clambered down the steep path, hurried around a boulder and came face to face with Colonel Ruddock.

The Colonel's blue eyes fixed themselves on his.

"Did you see anyone on the way?" he demanded.

BILL did not reply for a moment. He was looking at the pistol in the Colonel's hand, the long pistol with the bulge on the end which told of a Maxim silencer. So that was the noise. His glance fell on something beyond, a huddled, dirty, grey mass from which a naked foot stuck out awkwardly. He shuddered, and the sunshine overhead seemed to darken. Here was sudden death.

"No, not a soul, Colonel," he answered at last.

Colonel Ruddock slipped his weapon out of sight under his jacket and lit a cigarette. Bill stared at him in amazement. This was another Colonel Ruddock from the peaceful student he had known. His very voice, sharp and metallic now, was changed, fierce resolution was written in every line of his face.

"That man," said the Colonel, waving his hand toward the corpse, "was one of Haidar Ali's jackals. Do you know who Haidar Ali is?"

"Never heard of him."

"Other people have, though. He's the agent of His Highness, the Maharajah of Anar."

Bill nodded. "I've heard a bit about the Maharajah. Bazaar talk, of course. They say he isn't in too good with the Government just now. Trying to stir up trouble, and get more power for himself."

"Quite so. But listen to this. The Maharajah is a weakling. He doesn't matter. He may think he does, but he's wrong."

A thought struck Bill, and he grinned mirthlessly. Here was a high up Government official letting out the weaknesses of a ruling prince to him, to Bill Hicks, jailbird and embezzler. Three years ago, before the crash, it might have seemed ordinary enough. Now there was something almost funny in the idea.

His glance fell on the huddled body, and his grin vanished.

Colonel Ruddock's level voice went on.

"The man who really does matter is Haidar Ali. For years he has been making plans, very careful, intelligent, and well laid, to bring about a mass rising against the British rule."

Bill gasped. It was a big thing, then, almost too big to be true. He glanced suspiciously at the Colonel, but the calm, matter-of-fact tones continued.

"If he fails, the Maharajah will get the blame. If he succeeds, then the Maharajah will certainly meet with some accident, and Haidar Ali will seize the power."

"Yes, maybe," said Bill. "But for every native who's going to follow an unknown leader, there'll be a thousand who won't budge a step." His words were careless, but he felt a sudden chill. Where was this leading?

There was a flicker of approval in the Colonel's glance.

"Quite right. But Haidar Ali's name means more than you think He's a descendant of the Moghul Emperors, who once ruled in Delhi. They drenched those Northern cities in blood and paved them with gold in their day, and plenty of fools with empty pockets and old scores to settle may think that day may be coming again."

The Colonel paused, lit another cigarette, and continued.

"Two things make me believe we're getting near the crisis. One is that every hour more people know who Haidar Ali's ancestors really were. There behind me (pointing at the corpse) is the other. Haidar Ali has suspected me of watching him for some time, but only now has he begun to take steps to get rid of me. That fellow yonder has dogged me for days, waiting for his chance. I gave it to him just before you came."

BILL frowned. "You're probably right, sir, but where do I come in on all this?"

He had no need to ask. He knew, and the palms of his hands grew cold and moist.

"Haidar Ali must die," said the Colonel. "I can't use a native, because not one of them would lay a hand on the descendant of the Moghuls. The man's a murderer, but I've no shadow of evidence, so the police can't help me."

"Why don't you kill him yourself then?" asked Bill gruffly.

"I could, but who would ever believe it wasn't the Government which had given me the order? And that would make a martyr of the fellow. You know what a rising means. Blood, terror, hundreds of innocent folks killed, all because of one man."

"What sort of a chap is this Haidar Ali, anyway?"

"Thin, dark, rather slit-eyed. A cunning devil and a killer if he can do it safely. The only man he really trusts is a big negro, as cruel a brute as ever used a knife."

"You want me to kill Haidar Ali?" asked Bill hoarsely. There it was. He had known for the last five minutes really, and it meant almost certain death.

His eyes wandered to the corpse where carrion flies buzzed above a pool of blackening blood. Soon he would be like that. He shuddered. It was too much.

"I don't see how I can," he muttered.

Bill looked up at last and his eyes met the Colonel's. In them was understanding, pity, certainly, but also something else, something very like contempt. This was the end of the Colonel's belief in him. His thoughts ran on. What had he to lose, after all? What good was this kind of life, anyhow? And by risking it he could save thousands of people, get back some of the things he had lost maybe, and climb out of the pit into which that devil Feroz Shah had flung him.

He took a deep breath. Under the red bristles his mouth set in a grim line.

"I'll do it," he said quietly.

There was a long silence, broken by Bill.

"If Haidar Ali dies suddenly, what are the police going to do about it?"

"They've got to do their duty, of course. If the murderer leaves any clue they'll follow it up, and they're watching the house day and night. I was thinking, hoping perhaps you— Well, it needs to be a pretty well arranged crime, I suppose."

"Humph! I'll do my best."

There was a pause while the two men stared at each other. "If you do manage it," said the Colonel at last,

"I'll give—No, I won't promise you anything, but let me tell you this. I happen to know you didn't steal that money from your bank. You were framed."

Bill scowled. Somehow that didn't seem to matter.

"Never mind," he said. "It's over long ago. We needn't bring all that up. Let's fix up a few details of this Haidar Ali business while we can We may not be able to see each other again."

It was as well that neither of them could foresee the manner of their next meeting.

Clad in flowing white, Haidar Ali sat in the courtyard of his house reading and re-reading a note. His thoughts were none of the most pleasant. Mahmud, the spy, was dead, shot through the heart with a pistol. His body had been found hidden in a ravine near the skinners' bazaar, and footprints of two pairs of shod feet were near it.

He twisted the paper in his long white fingers and his eyes narrowed to gleaming slits. Colonel Ruddock had done the shooting, of course, for the spy had been hunting him. A clever man, the Colonel. But who was the other?

ONCE more he glanced at the note. "Makhsur, broken down," he read. One pair of shoes had been old, worn out, toes sticking out through the ends. That sounded like some poverty stricken half caste.

Voices inside the house 'roused him and the negro servant hurried into the courtyard, his face twitching with excitement. He grinned, and his white teeth, filed to sharp points, gave him the look of some savage beast of prey.

"Excellency, the mechanic from the garage has come," he announced. "He is working on the car now."

"Good." He waved dismissal, but the servant did not go.

"It is a white man, Excellency, tall,

with a red beard."

"What of it?"

"His shoes are very old, and broken at the ends."

Haidar Ali started.

"Footprints in the ravine, and now he comes here. It fits in well. You did right to tell me, Abdul. He may be an agent of the Colonel. If he is—" He paused, and a calculating look came over his face. "Well, it matters little. Perhaps we can find a use for him in any case."

Haidar Ali's slim white fingers tapped thoughtfully on the arms of his chair. Suddenly he sprang to his feet, his face alight with excitement.

"I have it!" he exclaimed. "See that the grey room is made ready and take the man there as soon as he leaves me. Clean the Afghan knife and put it in the room on the table. Be careful, be very careful. One finger mark on that knife and you are lost."

His eyes blazed with such a flame of hate and triumph that even the negro shuddered.

"Now, listen," he went on. Get ready a messenger. He must go to Colonel Ruddock, now, at once, with this letter."

He took a piece of paper, wrote a few lines, and gave it to the servant.

"The police are still watching the house?" he asked. "They are. Good. Go now, see to the other things and then bring me the mechanic. Search him first, and be sure he has no sort of arms."

In the cool gloom of the lower room where Haidar Ali's ancient Mercedes was kept, Bill was bending over his work. He had nearly finished when a voice made him jump to his feet. It came from behind him, and he turned to face the big negro.

"His Excellency wishes to see you at once," he said. Bill controlled himself with an effort. After all he was only

filing something. What could be more natural.

"All right. Let me get these things back in their places."

Cursing his luck, cursing that unseen door by which the man had come upon him, Bill put away his work and followed the servant. There was nothing else to be done.

When they had gone a few steps the man stopped Bill, felt in his pockets, and ran cunning hands over his clothing.

"What's this for?" he asked angrily, but there was no reply, and presently the big negro, satisfied, led him across the hall and among the pillars of the courtyard, into the presence of Haidar Ali.

"Excellency, the mechanic," he announced, and Haidar Ali rose from his chair.

For an instant the two men stared at each other. Then Bill's voice, thick and hoarse, broke the silence.

"The work is done." He could say no more. That face, the face that had haunted him through the years, pale, smiling, confident in its devilish cunning, was before him in the flesh. Haidar Ali, descendant of kings, and Feroz Shah, the bank clerk, were the same. The surprise was almost too great to control.

A SLOW flush rose to Haidar Ali's pale cheeks, and a venomous gleam flashed from his dark eyes, but Bill's own emotions kept him from seeing it. His thoughts were racing now. More than ever he must play this game to its bitter end. A terrible suspicion struck him. Had he been recognized?

He looked at Haidar Ali sharply and spoke.

"Excellency, it is a pity that none of your servants understand an automobile."

The pale face was like a mask, supercilious, a little weary, but without a sign of recognition.

Bill went on boldly.

"Surely your Excellency needs a strong servant who can do all that is necessary for an automobile, drive it, clean it, and keep it running smoothly."

Haidar Ali grinned.

"You wish to enter my service. Why?"

Bill shrugged his shoulders.

"I am poor. My wages are small, it is said your Excellency is generous."

Haidar Ali relaxed, but his hand was in his bosom, clutching something. Bill guessed what it was, and it did not make him any happier. Nevertheless, when the dark man spoke, his voice was mild.

"You may be useful to me. Go now and wait in the servants' quarters. I will consider your offer."

Bill turned and went out. He could feel Haidar Ali's glare boring into his shoulder blades, and he knew the hand still rested on the hidden weapon.

A voice at his elbow startled him.

"The master says you are to come to the little grey room and wait there."

There was something in the negro's look that Bill did not like, but he followed him in silence. The man unlocked a door and ushered him into a small square room. Bill turned to ask a question, but as he did so the door slammed, the lock clicked. He hurled himself against the stout wood, but it did not give. A low chuckle, and the sound of retreating footsteps. He was trapped.

Bill cursed fluently. Haidar Ali must have recognized him after all, and his talk about employing him was just a fake. He looked around. The room was dimly lit by a brass oil lamp high up in the vaulted roof. A rough wooden bed occupied one corner, a small table stood in another, and on the table lay something long and glittering. He went across and looked. It was a dagger of finest steel, with a smooth silver handle, and he reached out to pick it up, then stopped abruptly.

Why was that thing lying there? Did Haidar Ali expect him to commit suicide? No reason for that. Maybe they wanted him to kill somebody. Well, he wouldn't do it, that was all. Stories of the old Moghul Emperors came to Bill's mind, stories of men thrown to hungry tigers, with only a knife to fight off the ravenous brutes. Maybe something of the sort was going to happen to him. He shook his head. A dagger like that would give a strong man a sporting chance. Haidar Ali was not the kind to let an enemy have even that much advantage. There was something deeper and more subtle than that.

Bill prowled anxiously about the room. The stone of the tiny window sill was over a foot thick, sufficient to deaden any sound, even if he shouted all night. There was nothing to do but wait.

Slowly the minutes dragged. Twice Bill reached for the knife, and drew his hand away. That was what they wanted of him, to use it. The very thing he mustn't do.

Voices. A shuffle of feet, a clash of keys, and the door flew open In the doorway stood Haidar Ali with a leveled pistol.

"Dog," he said softly. "One move and you die." Then to the big negro. "Bring it in and lay it on the bed."

BENDING under his burden, the negro shuffled forward, dumped a long dark bundle on the planks, and unwrapped it.

Bill stared in horror. It was the body of a man, and the head wagged disjointedly, for the throat was cut from ear to ear Something in the ghastly face was familiar.

The negro undid the wrappings and bunched them together carefully. The man was newly dead, for the blood still flowed sluggishly from the severed arteries.

Bill stared wildly at Haidar Ali, but the pistol never wavered.

"Here, take this," Haidar Ali handed a bowl to the negro. "Sprinkle it on the bed and on our friend."

The negro obeyed. Warm liquid splashed on Bill's face and he jumped back.

"What is a little blood, after all," said Haidar Ali, chuckling.

Bill said nothing Frozen with horror he was looking at the dead face. Colonel Ruddock. Murdered! But why had they brought his body here?

"Lift the knife by the blade," said Haidar Ali to the negro. "On your life do not touch the hilt."

The man raised the dagger and looked toward his master.

"Now, very carefully, dip the cutting edge in the blood. It is well. Drop it there on the floor."

Suddenly Bill realized he was caught. All that remained was for Haidar Ali to call the police. To them he was a murderer, corpse, weapon there to hang him.

Haidar Ali saw the look on his face and laughed.

"Yes, my friend. You have guessed right. The justice of the English is swift and sure I shall get permission from His Excellency, the Governor, to see you hang, for the death of my friend the Colonel took place, alas in my poor house."

The door slammed, the key grated, and Bill was alone with the dead. Black fury welled up in him taking the place of horror. Vengeance on Haidar Ali. His own fate was nothing compared to this burning thirst to kill that hellish murderer. Screaming with rage, he beat on the wood with his fists.

In the distance a shrill whistle sounded, then another. He stopped.

The police. They would be here in a minute. What could he tell except the truth? And how could they believe him?

Heavy footsteps rang on the stone passage and a tall native inspector bustled in, followed by two constables. The inspector stared at the corpse for a moment and then turned to Bill. His look was cold, grimly appraising, and Bill's heart sank. The man was a Mohammedan, in Haidar Ali's pay as likely as not.

There was a long silence broken by Haidar Ali.

"Yes, inspector, my poor friend came to visit me and he entered this room by mistake. You can see what happened. This renegade Englishman must have had some grudge against him."

The innspector bowed politely.

"Doubtless it was as your Excellency relates, but—permit me."

He stepped forward, picked up the knife by the point, and turned to the constable.

"Ahmed, take the finger prints of all here and compare them with those on this knife."

The inspector studied the marks for a time, then turned to Haidar Ali with a smile.

"Has anyone but this man," pointing to Bill, been in the room since the Colonel entered?"

"My servant opened the door, saw what had happened, locked it, and ran for help. That was all."

The officer looked thoughtful for a moment, then he turned sharply to his subordinates.

"Arrest the negro," he said briskly, "and take him to the police station for questioning."

Haidar Ali's eyes blazed.

"I protest," he cried angrily. "How can you imagine that my servant could be connected with the crime?"

The inspector shrugged his shoulders.

"Excellency, I do not imagine. I see. The only fingerprints on the knife are those of your servant."

"Made long ago."

"No, for they are in blood, on the blade."

HAIDAR ALI pointed an accusing finger at Bill. "The fingerprints on the hilt must be those of that man."

"Pardon, Excellency." The inspector's voice was softly apologetic. "On the hilt are no fingerprints, none at all."

Haidar Ali choked, but said nothing. The inspector stared at him.

"Maybe others also will have be be questioned," he said. "If so, I shall send for them later, with your permission."

Haidar Ali turned away, and his eyes met Bill's. In his face was savage satisfaction, and his hand slipped toward his bosom. Bill understood. He and Haidar Ali were going to be left alone. A great relief welled up in him. His chance was coming. Somehow he would kill that stony hearted murderer. Vengeance lay before him like a shining goal.

The police marched off with their prisoner. As the outer door shut behind them Haidar Ali whipped out his pistol.

"Now, my friend," he said. "Walk before me. Down that passage. Turn to the right. Forward."

They went into the room where the big Mercedes stood and Bill's heart gave a jump. The work which he had done earlier in that very place was going to be useful after all. Haidar Ali intended to make him drive him outside the city to some lonely spot where he could kill him in safety. Well and good. Before that something would happen, something must, any minute now. His hands shook a little with suppressed excitement.

"Open those doors," came the order.

Bill flung them wide.

"Now lift the hood. See that the oil is sufficient."

The pistol's dark muzzle menaced Bill as he obeyed, but he scarcely noticed. He was thinking of the dead Colonel, and his muscles gathered themselves together like steel springs.

The police arrived in a hurry ten minutes later. Bill was still standing by Haidar Ali's body where it lay stabbed through the heart.

"Was it you who shouted for us?" demanded the officer, looking up from the corpse.

"Yes," said Bill quietly. "His Excellency, Haidar Ali, has been murdered. A tall, bearded Pathan did it with a knife and ran away. His Excellency fired one shot at him, but he missed."

"Where were you when it happened?"

"In the car, I had just started the engine."

The officer, a stout Hindu, put his hand on the radiator and nodded. All the same, he looked at Bill with dark suspicion.

"Arrest this man," he said, turning to a constable. "Search him, look in the car, look everywhere for a long, thin knife. We'll hunt for the fellow he talks about if we don't find it." He grunted with disgust. "What a pity the gate guard went with that negro; he would have been able to see the whole affair."

Bill heard the words dully. Somehow he no longer cared much about anything. He felt very tired.

The next morning saw Bill, pale and apathetic, about to be released. He hardly listened to the police officer's farewell words. He had had revenge, but somehow it mattered very little. He had saved a rising, brought safety to thousands. That was a heartening thought, but now the only man who knew and understood was dead.

HE sighed. What would happen when he went back to the bazaar? Evidence or not, none of Haidar Ali's followers would ever believe that he hadn't killed him. A knife in the back in a few short hours was the answer. Well, no man can escape fate. He shrugged his shoulders, and strode out into the sunshine.

An English voice roused him.

"Hi, Mr. Hicks." The speaker was a pleasant faced, grey haired man in uniform. He was sitting by the roadside on a pile of stone, and Bill turned toward him.

"I'm Colonel Jones," the stranger told him. "I heard about poor Ruddock and came over for a word with you. First of all, congratulations. You did a neat job with Haidar Ali and saved from the country from a terrible outburst."

Bill stared at him in surprise and the Colonel smiled.

"Some of us get knocked out of the game, but it still goes on," he continued. "Now, I want to make you an offer. Will you take the post of head clerk in the Intelligence Bureau at Simla? You crashed once, I know, but I also know why. You were a first class man before that, and there are still such things as responsibility and success, remember."

Bill gasped. Reputation, the respect of his fellow countrymen, all he had lost was coming back. He blinked mistily at the Colonel and stammered something about being grateful.

"Grateful, nothing," said the officer. "Only fair. The law took everything when you weren't guilty. You're going to get another chance now because you are. By the way, where did hide the knife?"

"It wasn't a knife. I sharpened the oil measurer out of the car and used it. That is why I had to start the engine to make the oil wash the blood off after I put it back."

The Colonel smiled. "You will make a most intelligent head clerk," he said.

STATEMENT OF THE OWNERSHIP, MANAGEMENT, CIRCULATION, ETC., REQUIRED BY THE ACT OF CONGRESS OF MARCH 3, 1933

Of Ka-Zar, Published Bi-Monthly at Chicago, Ill., for October 1, 1936.

State of New York }
County of New York } ss.

Before me, a Notary Public in and for the State and county aforesaid, personally appeared Charles Goodman, who, having been duly sworn according to law, deposes and says that he is the Editor of the Ka-Zar and that the following is, to the best of his knowledge and belief, a true statement of the ownership, management (and if a daily paper, the circulation), etc., of the aforesaid publication for the date shown in the above caption, required by the Act of August 24, 1912, embodied in section 411, Postal Laws and Regulations, printed on the reverse of this form, to wit:

1. That the names and addresses of the publisher, editor, managing editor, and business managers are: Publisher, Manvis Publications, Inc., RKO Bldg., Radio City, New York. Editor, Charles Goodman, RKO Bldg., Radio City, New York. Managing Editor, Charles Goodman, RKO Bldg., Radio City, New York. Business Manager, Martin Goodman, RKO Bldg., Radio City, New York.

2. That the owner is: (If owned by a corporation, its name and address must be stated and also immediately thereunder the names and addresses of stockholders owning or holding one per cent or more of total amount of stock. If not owned by a corporation the names and addresses of the individual owners must be given. If owned by a firm, company, or other unincorporated concern, its name and address, as well as those of each individual member, must be given.) Manvis Publications, Inc., RKO Bldg., Radio City, New York. Charles Goodman, RKO Bldg., Radio City, New York. Jean Davis Goodman, RKO Bldg., Radio City, New York.

3. That the known bondholders, mortgagees, and other security holders owning or holding 1 per cent or more of total amount of bonds, mortgages, or other securities are: (If there are none, so state.) None.

4. That the two paragraphs next above, giving the names of the owners, stockholders, and security holders, if any, contain not only the list of stockholders and security holders as they appear upon the books of the company but also, in cases where the stockholder or security holder appears upon the books of the company as trustee or in any other fiduciary relation, the name of the person or corporation for whom such trustee is acting, is given; also that the said two paragraphs contain statements embracing affiant's full knowledge and belief as to the circumstances and conditions under which stockholders and security holders who do not appear upon the books of the company as trustees, hold stock and securities in a capacity other than that of a bona fide owner; and this affiant has no reason to believe that any other person, association, or corporation has any interest direct or indirect in the said stock, bonds, or other securities than as so stated by him.

5. That the average number of copies of each issue of this publication solid or distributed, through the mails or otherwise, to paid subscribers during the twelve months preceding the date shown above is..........(This information is required from daily publications only.)

CHARLES GOODMAN.
(Signature of editor, publisher, business manager, or owner.)

Sworn to and subscribed before me this 1st day of October, 1936.
[SEAL]

MAURICE COYNE.
(My commission expires March 30, 1938.)

Notary Public, Bronx Co. No. 90. Reg. No. 52-C-38. Cert. filed in N. Y. Co. No. 500, Reg. No. 8-C-265. Cert. filed in Kings Co. No. 144, Reg. No. 8210. Commission expires March 30, 1938.

*H*ADES' *R*EEF

by Norman A. Daniels

The daring Americano with more nerve than caution wages a fight to the finish against the perils of Brazil.

SLIM STUART hoisted himself out of his easy chair and cocked his head to one side. Above him he could hear the rhythmic clicking of the lighthouse apparatus that keep the huge lamp blinking. Striving to stifle this sound the waves rolled in over Hades' Reef as if in anger at the man-made tower that cheated it of its prey. Yet, above all this Slim could have sworn he heard a shout.

He slipped into a well worn reefer and stepped out of the lighthouse. Somewhere in the blackness that hemmed in the tiny portion of land was Ramon Ortego, his young assistant.

"Ramon — hey Ramon," Slim shouted, cupping his hands to make the sound carry. "Where the devil are you?"

There was no reply. Slim broke into a dog trot and ran down the treacherous rock incline to the small wharf that jutted out over the sea. Ramon had gone there to tie up the surf boat which the Brazilian government fondly believed capable of taking a man back to the mainland in event of emergency. He walked across the wharf, bending his body away from the wind and holding his pipe between hard clamped teeth. The surf boat was there all right.

Slim pulled a flashlight from his pocket and turned its ray on the hitch that held the painter to the wharf. There was a peculiar knot in it—one that Ramon was accustomed to fashioning. Slim thought back swiftly. He had used the boat to do a little fishing and tied it up several hours before. That meant Ramon had untied it and retied it again, probably to be certain that it was secure.

Slim grunted and as he arose the path of his flash swept across the wooden surface of the wharf. It stopped dead and centered in its ray was the wet imprint of a man's foot. Only the left one was visible for the waves had swept across a portion of the wharf already. But that one footprint made him start visibly. It was abnormal for the little toe was missing.

Then Slim gave vent to a lusty curse. Two feet from the footprint was a smear of blood. He tested it with his finger and found it fresh, not yet congealed. Even as he tried to figure this out a wave sent a spray over the boards and the footprint and blood smear were erased as if by some giant hand.

He stepped closer to the edge and brought the beam of his light down into the water. Two evil shapes slipped by and an upturned white belly flashed for a second.

"God help him if he fell in there," Slim muttered. "But he wasn't a careless lad and he could swim like a fish."

Slim gave up after two hours of careful searching. He covered every inch of the tiny island and there was no sign of Ramon. Back in the warmth and comfort of the lighthouse, Slim fished out four signal flares. Two were red, one yellow and the other white. He got out the rocket pistol and sat down to wait until the light fog died away. It was far into the early morning hours when he stepped to the shore, raised the pistol and fired the four rockets. They burst high in the air and on the mainland keen eyes spotted them and read their meaning.

At noon the next day Slim was haggard of face and his eyes were bloodshot from twenty-four hours of constant duty. It had been Ramon's night shift, but Slim had to assume it when the young Brazilian vanished. He fixed a telescope to his eye and peered out over the reef. A small Brazilian gunboat was dropping her anchor and two boats were being let down the davits.

It took almost an hour before the first boat beached on the rocks and Slim stepped into the sea almost to the top of his high boots and helped the naval lieutenant to shore.

"We received your signal, Señor Stuart," the lieutenant bowed slightly. "Something has happened, *si?*"

"It has," Slim declared gloomily. "I hope your signal corps read my message right. I sent up a yellow flare asking for an assistant. I don't see him."

"He comes in the second boat, amigo. But what has happened to Ramon? He is ill, perhaps?"

"He's dead. Ramon went out last night to tie up the surf boat and—he didn't come back. I noticed sharks in the water near the wharf. He must have fallen in and those devils made short work of him."

"Ah—sad—so sad," the lieutenant shook his head sorrowfully. "Ramon was a good boy—and a brave one. We brought the supplies a week ahead of time, amigo, so we should not have to come to this forsaken spot for three more months. But here comes your new assistant. May he have better fortune than Ramon."

SLIM watched as a chunky, ape-like man stepped from the prow of the second boat and walked briskly toward them. He was a Brazilian and his dark features were none too prepossessing.

He had thick lips and squinty eyes that couldn't stay still.

"This is Pedro Carrubba, amigo. Now I must go—at once. There has been trouble close to Brazil. One of our sister nations overcame a revolution, but much blood was spilled and the revolutionists are fleeing the land. They seek to enter Brazil, but we have orders to keep them out, so we are very busy. So, Señor — adios. In three months I will return and I trust everything will be satisfactory."

He saluted, bowed with the politeness of a South American and returned to his boat. He waved as the husky arms of his sailors sent the craft cleaving the water toward the small gunboat.

"I have heard of you, Senor Stuart," Pedro broke the quiet. "The fame of the Norte Americano has spread to all of Brazil. It takes a brave man to operate this devil's own lighthouse. I go now—to examine the lamp."

"Hop to it," Slim rubbed his chin, "but on your way pick up some of *these* crates and lug 'em with you. By the look of your muscles you won't break your back with 'em."

Pedro glowered momentarily like a man who hated orders. But he shrugged, bent over and hoisted a heavy box of canned goods to his shoulder. Slim barely stifled a gasp for as Pedro bent down, his coat was whipped away from his body by the wind and for a second the butt of a heavy gun was revealed.

"Now what," Slim asked himself as he eyed the Brazilian's retreating back, "does he want with a gun on this forsaken place?"

He sighed, picked up an armful of supplies and followed Pedro into the lighthouse. The Brazilian stood looking about.

"Ah, amigo, you have the fine place here, no? Three months will not be so bad for Pedro, I think. I have a look at the barometer. It falls rapidly, senor.

There is a storm breaking tonight?"

"By the looks of things I'd say she was going to be a bad one," Slim nodded. "Probably fog too. There was some last night—when Ramon slipped off that wharf. You watch yourself, Pedro. If you ain't used to climbing around wet rocks, it might be dangerous. But come along. I'll show you how to clean the reflectors and the blinds. That's your first job."

At dinner Pedro shovelled food into his mouth. He wiped his lips with the back of his hand and grinned.

"The storm—it is coming quickly, senor. The fog too—already it is difficult to see the reefs. Should the light not penetrate the fog, then you start the bell, eh?"

"I'll show you how to do that too," Slim said. "She'll have to start tolling in about an hour. This pea soup is bad around here and the reefs hard to spot. If you're done, we'll start. Take off your shoes and socks, man. It's better to crawl around with your naked feet."

Pedro shrugged and obeyed. Together they stiffened themselves against the velocity of the wind. Above, the lighthouse was functioning perfectly. The sweeping light lent a little cheerfulness to the island.

"This is a bad place to be caught in a storm, eh, amigo?" Pedro asked.

"They named the reef Hades Reef," Slim replied, shouting against the wind. "There's a deep water channel between this reef and another one a mile out. The ships steer a course between the rocks and the light and bell guide them. See that little house? That's where the levers that start and stop the bell are kept. That little runway goes out to the rock where the bell is suspended. Maybe you better take a walk out there and see if it's fastened tight."

Pedro looked askance at the slender, treacherous cat walk over which swept the spray from the waves. He glanced at Slim, shrugged and stepped to the plank. As he moved out over the sea, Slim's flashlight dropped a little. He started in amazement. Pedro had stepped directly on the wet plank. His footprints were held in bold relief for a moment before water washed them away.

The little toe of the left foot was missing!

PEDRO returned after a few moments and his face was livid with fright. He stepped to the shore, looked back at the howling sea and shivered.

"A bad place, senor. It is the devil's own, this lighthouse.

"You can stow that," Slim said firmly. "Get back into the lighthouse. And you might tell me what you did to poor Ramon last night."

"What I did to Ramon? Last night?" Pedro turned with a puzzled frown on his face. "I do not comprehend, senor."

"You know what I mean well enough. You stepped on that wharf last night and left your trade mark. A man with his little toe missing should be more careful."

Pedro's eyes narrowed to mere slits. The intermittent beam of the huge lamp reflected against the thick fog and Slim saw every cruel line of that broad face. The Brazilian's right hand crept behind him. Slim lurched forward. His foot slipped on the slimy rock and he went down, arms flailing in their vain attempt to grasp Pedro and pull him down too.

Pedro laughed as Slim picked himself up only to look into the important end of a heavy revolver.

"You are clever, amigo," Pedro granted. "Too clever to live long. We go back to the lighthouse after you start the big bell tolling. Should you be so foolish as to attack me, I shall kill you, pronto."

Slim said nothing. He kept his hands shoulder high, walked to the little shed and jammed down the starting lever. Out on the rock the big bell began to sway. Its sweep became greater and greater until finally the clapper struck the resonant sides with a terrific gong.

With Pedro's gun in the small of his back, Slim led the way back to the lighthouse. Distantly he could hear the bellow of a ship's siren and as if in reply, the giant bell boomed out its warning note.

"We shall wait—here," Pedro smiled evilly. "Perhaps you can be of use to us, amigo, and by our grace you may yet live many years."

"Maybe you wouldn't mind explaining this piece of black work, you shifty-eyed renegade," Slim said softly. "And you'll get no help from me—not' if I have to die for it."

"So?" Pedro raised his eyebrows in mock surprise. "The senor will not play. This is too bad. Soon my friends will be here. Then we shall see."

For twenty minutes Slim sat in grim silence and not for one instant did his eyes leave those of the Brazilian. But Pedro was patient too and his gun didn't waver.

The sound of a hull scraping against rock brought the thick set traitor to his feet. He backed to the door, opened it and without turning his head raised his voice in a shout.

Answering hails reached him. Soon the tramp of feet announced the arrival of Pedro's cohorts. Three men, dripping wet, walked into the lighthouse. One of them was a pompous, obese man with a curling mustachio and a heavy gun buckled around his clothing. Pedro bowed to him, but he kept his gun pointed toward Slim.

" 'sta bueno, mi general," he said. "This pig of an Americano was as simple to handle as those fools of Brazilian naval officers!"

"Before this night is over," the

pompous man said, "we shall succeed with craft where bullets and blood failed. But we must hurry."

Pedro walked over to Slim and pushed him into the easy chair. He levelled the gun at his chest and slowly his thumb pulled back the hammer.

"You will talk, si? There is, in the deep water channel, a ship which must not pass. You will tell us where to place another bell—like the one tolling now—so this ship will be drawn on the rocks."

"Do you mean to tell me you're going to wreck a ship?" Slim asked in amazement. "What are you—pirates?"

"No—we are insurrectos. Aboard that ship is a man we wish to kill. For months we sought to assassinate him, but he is too careful for that. Even a revolution failed. Now we shall kill him here."

"Then you'll get no information out of me," Slim declared flatly. "You can do your devil's work on me, but I'm not going to send that ship on the rocks. Not for you nor any other of your kind."

PEDRO snorted, turned to the pudgy general and talked in a low voice. Finally he pulled a long, keen knife from a leg holster. He stepped close to Slim and the point of the blade pricked his throat until the blood came and ran down in a thin, wavy line across his skin.

"It would be unfortunate to slit so nice a throat, senor. Perhaps you have reconsidered, yes?"

Slim's eyes narrowed. Pedro was close — comfortably close — but that knife was already pressing against his windpipe. Slim curled his fingers into tight fists and waited. Pedro scowled and removed the point of the knife. Slim's right fist came flying upward. It caught the treacherous South American full on the point of the jaw. Pedro was lifted clear off his feet and hurled against the wall. He slumped to the floor, his eyes glazed.

"Take him," the pudgy revolutionist leader snapped. His two aides drew guns and lunged forward with them. One cracked down on Slim's head. His senses reeled and before he could recover his wits, he was helpless.

Pedro dragged himself to his feet and carefully tested his jaw.

"Next time," Slim promised him, "I'll take the pleasure of breaking it."

"Next time — there will be no next time," Pedro roared. He picked up his knife, stepped close and with a flick of the point snapped the buttons from Slim's shirt. His chest was exposed. With a cruel smile Pedro began to press the point of the blade against the skin. Carefully, like an artist, he began to draw it through the surface flesh. Warm blood flowed down to saturate Slim's shirt, but his mouth was grimly set and his head high.

"Perhaps," the general broke in, "we should kill him, pronto, and fix the bell at once."

"We do not know this reef," Pedro disagreed. "The dog will do as I command. Look down, Senor Stuart. Look at your own blood. My little knife cuts deep, no? It can cut even deeper—like this."

An involuntary groan escaped from Slim's tight lips and Pedro smiled.

"A hundred thousand deaths you will suffer, amigo, unless you tell us where to affix the bell. Quickly now—we can wait no longer."

Slim thought swiftly. The mere silencing of the big bell that tolled its warning message just off the reef was enough to beach any ship already in the channel and they would certainly stop it. If he could stall them, something might happen."

"I'll do as you ask," he said. "If you'll fasten your bell to the rocks leeward of that reef, you'll draw the best captain along the coast on the rocks."

"Bueno, muy bueno," Pedro grinned. "You are wise, my friend. Perhaps you will die quickly now. If you are lying —Por Dios, I shall cut you to ribbons."

The pudgy general gave orders. Pedro and one of the other men raced out of the lighthouse and down to the small boat they had launched on the little island. Slim was alone with the general and one guard who kept his gun levelled and his eyes open. The general parked himself on the edge of the table, bit off the tip of an evil looking cigar and carefully scratched a match across the shiny table top.

"I've a pipe on that desk." Slim motioned with his head. "You wouldn't begrude a dying man a smoke?"

"But no." The general smiled, arose and picked up Slim's pipe. He threw it into the American's lap. Slim carefully tamped tobacco into the pipe, but unseen by either the general or the guard he also palmed a good handful of the finely cut tobacco. The guard walked warily toward him, gun extended. He threw a match toward Slim and stepped back a pace.

Slim took a long breath. The big bell was dying out now. Pedro had stopped it. Aboard that ship in the channel a worried captain would order the motors stopped until the tolling began again. The beam of the lighthouse penetrated the fog for only a short distance, valueless in soupy weather like this. Then, the moment Pedro and his men set up the other bell, the ship's motors would resume their beat. The pilot would turn the helm inland. There would be a sinister scraping of hull against rock. Then a terrific crash. The ship would go down as if weighted with lead.

SLIM raised one foot, scraped the match and held the flame to the bowl of his pipe. He puffed slowly, re-

moved the match and waved it in a perfectly natural manner of a man trying to extinguish the flame. But his hand jerked out. The tobacco flew into the eyes of the armed guard. The gun exploded and lead ripped into the wall behind Slim. The general turned and streaked for the door. Slim was after him like a flash.

The guard was tenderly rubbing his eyes and groping for the gun he had dropped. Slim grabbed the general around the waist, dragged him to the floor and snapped two healthy haymakers to the chin. The general groaned once and was still.

On his feet again, Slim faced the guard. The man had recovered his gun and was trying to draw a bead for the fatal shot. Slim's hand closed around a bottle of brass polish which he had placed on the floor. It hurtled across the room and found its mark between the gunman's eyes. Before he could recover from this blow, Slim was upon him. He wrapped his hands around the man's throat and squeezed. Rage surged through his usually calm mind. He bent the man backward and waited until his limbs went limp. Then he flung him to the floor, bent down and scooped up the gun he had dropped.

He raced for the door and as he went through it, the bell set up by Pedro, began its clanging. As if in reply the ship in the channel tooted cheerfully.

Slim groaned and ran toward the wharf. He made a line for the shed where the controls of the real bell were housed. As he reached it, two figures sprang out of the fog. Both held guns. Orange streaks of light broke through the fog. Slim felt a bullet bite the flesh of his left thigh, but he paid little heed to it. His purloined gun blasted and one of the men went down, face flat against the wooden wharf.

But the other man was Pedro. There had been more revolutionists waiting at the water's edge. They had set up the false bell while Pedro watched for the doomed ship.

"You can start dealing out those thousand deaths," Slim taunted the man. "I'm coming for you, Pedro, and it won't be a gun I'll use on your stinking hide. I'll use my bare hands and you'll wish it was a bullet before I'm through."

While he talked, Slim hedged toward the shed. His objective was the mechanism that would start the real bell tolling. If he could start it, the officers on the ship that Pedro wanted to wreck, would suspect mischief at once and stop. There was no other way to save them.

Intent on the shed, Slim crouched as he neared it. His gun was held at his hip, the hammer back with his thumb fanning it. The shed loomed up two feet before him. He reached out to grasp the latch of the door. There was a scuffling sound behind him and two hundred pounds of solid humanity came down on his back. Pedro grunted lurid curses and swung his gun. The barrel raked across Slim's face and drew blood.

Grimly he dropped his own weapon, reached up behind him and grasped Pedro's arm. With a terrific yank he brought the heavy Spaniard up and over. Pedro landed flat on his back, his legs dangling into the water. Instantly one of the sleek grey shapes materialized out of the fog. Pedro gave vent to a ghastly scream. His body slipped over the edge while his shrieks cut the thick air.

Slim grabbed the gun Pedro had dropped. Hastily he emptied it into the water. A wild swirling gave evidence to his marksmanship. Pedro was still screaming as Slim dragged him to safety. Slim sped toward the shed. He opened the door, grabbed the lever and yanked it down. Somewhere out in the fog he could hear the giant bell begin swaying. It squealed in its davits. Then the clapper struck the side. The clang almost split Slim's eardrums, but never had the bell sounded better to him.

In the channel the ship's siren wailed dolefully. Slim saw a crimson rocket explode in the air, its color making a red haze out of the fog. A landing party was being put overside.

When the three boats pulled up on the beach, Slim was waiting. Sailors sprang out, rifles levelled. A dapper officer walked briskly up to Slim. In angry words he demanded an explanation.

"Come along and I'll show you," Slim said quietly. "You're not hearing things, mister. Those are two bells clanging away, but only one of 'em is the real thing. The other was meant to lure your ship on the rocks."

"But I do not understand?" the officer cried.

WITH two squad of sailors at his heels, Slim led the way to the lighthouse. He flung open the door and the officer stepped inside. The revolutionist general was slowly recovering consciousness.

"Por Dios," the officer cried. "It is Sebastian—the man we have sought for weeks."

"I don't know what he's called," Slim said, "but you'll find the rest of his gang outside. One of 'em—his name is Pedro Carrubba, has part of his leg chewed off by a shark. I saved him. For what I don't know—he tried hard enough to murder me."

"Pedro Carrubba," the naval officer breathed softly. "Ah, senor, you have done a great service for my nation this night. I understand now. Aboard my ship, in the channel, is el Presidente. Sebastian and Pedro sought to assassinate him so they might get control of my government. They failed and we believed them either dead or escaped to Mexico. Their spies told them el presidente was on his way north and his ship would have to enter this channel. They planned to wreck the ship and kill him when he tried to land. Gracias, Senor, for the great service. You shall be rewarded."

"To the devil with the reward," Slim grinned happily. "Just clear my little reef of these carrion. They must have a ship some place out in the channel. Maybe you can spot her. And don't forget Pedro. Pick out the dirtiest cell you can find and throw him in."

"But no, amigo," the officer smiled. "For Pedro there is only a brick wall and rifles at dawn."

"Still he had nerve," Slim said thoughtfully. "He killed Ramon so he could come here as relief man. He probably bribed some official of the Brazilian government for the job. He figured I'd be easy to handle and when the general pulled into port, things would be ready. Now get the rats off. The fog is lifting and I've got to tend my light."

Slim was adjusting the reflectors when he heard the crashing of light naval guns somewhere beyond the channel. The government ship had found the renegade vessel all right. Slim grinned. Tending a lighthouse wasn't so monotonous after all.

WHITE DEVILS

by R. A. Emberg

On mysterious Papeete, the good deed that Don Prince once did for a native is returnd with interest and when most needed.

DON PRINCE, twenty years old, blue eyed, disillusioned and very very homesick for San Francisco, sat on the wharf at Papeete and watched the La Belle Francais poke her nose toward the wharf. Passengers crowding the steamer's forepeak thrilled to the zip of brown bodies as bronzed boys dived for coins. Suddenly a tensed hush as a long dorsal fin broke water. It cruised in the midst of the swimmers. In a wink the stringpieces and piles were cluttered with dripping forms as the native swimmers shinned upward.

One still remained in the water, Narri, the south sea tramp, come from where, no one knew, and the shark's fin was very near. Narri's head broke water. He screamed, the scream dying as he was dragged under.

It's news when a man bites a dog and by the same token, something out of the ordinary when a Caucasion, a very blonde one at that, rescues a Kanaka from death in the water. That's exactly what happened.

Prince never knew what prompted him, perhaps the knowledge that he once swam the Golden Gate, perhaps a sort of a fraternal instinct, Narri was a friendless stranger in Papeete also, but whatever it was, he drew a sailor's sheath knife from his tattered dungarees and plunged off the wharf.

With powerful strokes, he made his way to the churning white froth. A slaty bulk loomed ahead and under. He raised the knife. It came down, vicious, hard, digging deep. Again and again. And yet again. The white froth reddened. With a limp, bleeding Narri in tow, Prince struck out for the dock. Hands reached for him, took his burden and helped him up. Panting, he sat on a pile and gazed at the boy he had rescued. Flesh in shreds hung from thigh to knee. Brown Polynesian eyes looked gratefully into blue American ones. Narri smiled through his pain.

"Name belong you?" he asked.

"Don Prince," the American returned.

"Me," tapping his chest, "Narri. My name belong you. Your name belong me. You—Narri, me," slurring the words t o g e t h e r, "Donprince. We brothers."

The gendarmes took Narri away to the hospital. That evening Prince shipped on a Sydney bound schooner. In time, the incident became simply a memory. Ten years slipped by.

THE Kanaka helmsman put the wheel down, the Hiaa slipped into the wind and righted to an even keel. Her headsheets emptied and the reef points beat a stacatto chorus as she hung quivering. With a boathook, Don Prince, no longer a homesick youth of twenty, but one of the best liked men in the south seas, and owner and master of the schooner, reached over the side and hooked onto the dugout in which the form of a man sprawled.

"Bear a hand," he ordered the mate, "he's either dead or unconscious."

The mate hung onto the boathook while Prince slipped over the rail. A heave of his powerful shoulders and the castaway was aboard. Prince followed. The dugout was cast adrift, orders were rasped, boom tackles shifted and the Hiaa filled away.

The skipper and the mate worked over the man. Prince placed an ear to his bare chest. "Living all right," he said, "but that's all. Tehaa," he called, "bring water—rum—quick."

The big Kanaka cook came on the run with two bottles.

Prince opened the locked jaws and moistened a black parched tongue and mouth with a mixture of rum and water. He bathed the man's head. Finally the castaway opened his eyes.

"Water—Dios—water," he babbled. His eyes were blank—unseeing.

"Delirious," Prince said. "Take him to the focsle and put him in a bunk.

Thompson, the new mate shipped at Tahuata came aft. He was a bulky blond with tousled hair, strong yellow horse teeth and an unsavoury reputation. Not in a million years would Prince have shipped him had not Jock Cameron gone on a spree at Tahuata and failed to show up before sailing time.

Prince nodded at the focsle. "Been adrift for a long time," he said. "Make anything of him?"

Thompson shook his head. "Naw," he answered callously, "he'll die or I miss my guess. He's burnt to hell and gone."

THE sun had dropped behind the western rim of the ocean. Prince was pacing the poop, his eye on the draw of the mains'l when Tehaa padded alongside.

"Sick man say cap'n come," he said, flicking a finger for'ard.

Followed by the cook, Prince went to the focsle.

The dim light of a swinging oil lantern cast flickering light patterns on two tiers of empty bunks. The focsle was deserted except for the castaway. When the weather was decent the watch below slept on the forepeak.

The man was conscious and lucid, but death was on him. It rattled in his throat. He knew it.

"I am die, capitan," he whispered with a strong Spanish accent as Prince bent over him. "I no tell thees to anybody, but I have leetle girl—my babee — in Valparasio — at convent of St. Ursula. You hear—queeck, capitan—?"

"Aye," Prince nodded. "I hear."

"Me," the man continued, "I am one-time presidente—Beunaterra. Come revolution—I go on boat weeth much moneey—two hundred thousand dollars —Americano—gold. Rebel sheep chase me—you un'erstan'?"

"Yes—yes," Prince was all ears.

"My boat seenk off island—we get ashore — much fight weeth natives. Some keel—some steel there—an' gol' is een sheep one mile off shore. You fin'—take half—give rest to sisters— St. Ursula for my babee. Weel you do thees, capitan?"

For a moment Prince thought the man was still delirious, but the black eyes sunken deep into bony orbits blazed with the determination to impress.

"This island," he asked, "where is it?"

"Ben' closer, capitan—I am always suspect. Then only you weel hear."

Prince placed an ear to the man's mouth.

"The islan'—she ees—"

"Wait." There was the sound of a guarded movement in the focsle. Prince turned to see the bulky mate.

"What is it, Thompson?" he snapped.

"Nothing, captain, just came down to see the sick man. I didn't know you were here."

"Get back on deck," Prince ordered.

Listening till steps on the ladder told that Thompson had obeyed, he again placed his ear near the castaway's mouth.

"The island, where is it?" he asked.

He waited for a reply, but none came. He put an ear to the man's heart. It was still. The ex-presidente of Beunaterra was dead and the secret of the island had died with him.

"Passed out," Prince told Thompson a few minutes later on deck. "Have him sewed up in sail cloth and we'll drop him over. He won't keep till we make Papeete. Poor devil."

"Heard him say something about an island and two hundred thousand dollars?" Thompson's green eyes bored into Prince. "What's the dope?"

"He was president of Beunaterra," Prince answered. "Revolution and he had to skip. Took the federal funds with him. Chased by rebel gunboat and his ship went down off some island with all the money. Got a kid in a convent at Valparaiso. Died before he could tell me where the island is—"

"Yeah," Thompson said scoffingly.

Prince glanced at him. "What do you mean?" he asked.

"By what?" Thompson countered.

"By that yeah?"

"I don't believe you. If he told you that much, he told you the rest. That's why you ordered me out of the focsle. You're holding out."

Prince shrugged his shoulders. "No insubordination, mister," h e s a i d shortly. "Get him sewed up and let me know when he's ready." He walked aft.

The mate's eyes followed. He walked to leeward and squirted a mouthful of tobacco juice over the side. "Want to hog it, you blankety blank," he muttered. "But you have another think coming, Captain Prince."

THE Hiaa was berthed. Kanaka stevedores were busy at her hatches. Thompson who had been ashore climbed the rail and came to Prince.

"I'm leaving," he said shortly. "Pay me off and I'll have my stuff over the side."

"Sure," Prince agreed. "You signed articles for the voyage, but that's all right. I'll be able to ship a mate in your place. You're sore because you think I'm holding out on that island. Hell, man, the tale means nothing to me. I can't chase every will-o'-the-wisp that crosses my course. I'm in the trading business."

"Pay me off," Thompson growled.

Prince's gaze followed the man as he stamped away from the wharf. The thought that had been pricking him since the night the Beunaterran had died returned to plague him.

Two hundred thousand dollars was a lot of money; more than he'd make in a hundred years packing copra and shell. Of course there was the kid at Valparaiso; she's come in for half and if any of the president's crew were still alive, they too were entitled to a cut, but the residue was a darn tidy sum. Hell! he attempted to dismiss the thought. Even if the tale had been true, where was the island? How long had the dugout been adrift? Weeks, perhaps months. And there were only about ten million islands between the coast of South America and the spot where the Hiaa had picked it up.

But were there? He drew a mental picture of the Hiaa's position that afternoon. A line bisecting the 12th parallel of south latitude half way between the Marquesas and Arutua would pass over the spot.

He went to the cabin, dug up charts, current tables and a directory of the South Pacific, spread them on the table and reached for a pair of dividers.

"Let's see now," he muttered as he plotted the probable drift of the dugout. "Might have come from here," dotting a group of flyspecks, "or here,"

the point of the dividers rested on another group, "but so far as I know, they're uninhabited — only guano deposits and he spoke of natives." Then suddenly remembering that the seasonal change for the northwest monsoon and its accompanying weather tantrums had occurred a week prior to picking up the dugout, he shoved the charts away. "Can't tell where it drifted from," he growled.

He went on deck and gave orders to the Rappa bosun. Then he climbed over the side and headed for the American Consulate.

"WHAT do you know about Beunaterra?" Prince asked when the formal greeting were over.

The consul looked at him quizzically. He stirred the contents of the tall glass.

"Dinkey republic between Chile and Peru," he answered languidly. "Land of perpetual revolutions. The ins today are the outs tomorrow—and vice versa. So far as I know, the latest revolution was last January. Presidente Carlos Sanchez flew the coop with the Beunaterran treasury. He was refused permission to land anywhere on the west coast of South America and he headed this way with a rebel gunboat after him. That March twister must have gotten him. He never did show up, although the rebel, by that time, a federal, put in here the spring after combing the whole south Pacific. Seems to be a hell of a lot of interest in Beunaterra lately. Fellow came in this morning and wanted some information about the country."

"A husky blond with horse teeth?" Prince asked.

"Yeah," the consul retorted. "Know him?"

"He was my mate."

About to board the Hiaa on his return, Prince's eye caught the trim lines of a white schooner yacht anchored a few hundred feet away. He recognized her immediately. Bill Turlock's Sea Nymph. Her name belied her and her owner's reputation. British, French and American colonial administrators would have given a good deal to have gotten the goods on Turlock. He was suspected of every crime in the category of the south seas, ranging from outlawed black birding to pearl poaching. But he'd never been caught with his shirt off. He came and went to the unconcealed chagrin of port officials from Manila to Sydney and from Auckland to Honolulu.

Prince knew the man and his ship only by sight. He'd never met Turlock. As he watched, two men came over her rail. One was Turlock, broad chested, a veritable mountain of a man, in his early forties; the other was a husky tousle headed blond with horse teeth.

Prince whistled. "Thompson! And he's as chummy with Turlock as though they were blood brothers. A damned good pair."

Back in the cabin, he went over the charts again. After several hours work the points of the dividers rested on several dots a few hundred miles east of Raroia. "It's a hell of a long way from South America," he said to himself, "but it's worth a try and I'm giving it a whirl."

THOUGH his agent offered Prince a cargo and damned him when he wouldn't take it, the Hiaa left Papeete in ballast. A run back to Tahuata—he hoped Jock Cameron was over his spree; the mate was a good man except when on a periodical jag—then southeast in quest of that two hundred thousand dollars.

Without cargo and with the knowledge that Cameron would rejoin the schooner, Prince dispensed with shipping a mate at Papeete. The Rappa bosun could take the deck if necessary.

With a free sheet and a stiff breeze, the Hiaa threaded the coral patches and surged up smooth water to the Tahuata anchorage.

Cameron was there. He was contrite. More than that he was broke flatter than the proverbial pancake and very much in bad with the gendarmes.

Prince grinned as Cameron pleaded for his old berth. He vowed on his covenanting honor to never again look at a rum bottle. Prince had heard the same story so many times that it was no longer a novelty.

Then he almost forgot the tongue lashing he had promised himself to give Cameron. Less than two hours after the Hiaa had anchored, the Sea Nymph nosed in and let her hook go almost alongside.

"That was damned funny," Prince thought as he cast an appraising glance at the schooner. Had she tailed him clear across the Societies—? The answer flashed into his mind as a tousle headed blond materialized on the Sea Nymph's deck and a harsh voice rasped orders to the Kanaka crew. It was Thompson, apparently one of the afterguard. Turlock's pursuit of the Hiaa was premeditated and not merely a coincidence. Thompson had told him of the dead Beunaterran and the money. The south sea vulture was waiting to get in on the kill.

"He'll hang on like a leech wherever we go," Prince explained to Cameron. "I hate like hell to run away, but it's the best policy. Tonight, we'll douse our lights and tow out. If Turlock follows we'll return to the anchorage and wait. He'll have to tip his hand sooner or later."

An early morning found the Hiaa close hauled off the coast of a large island two hundred miles east of Low Archipelago. It had been a month and a half since that night at Tahuata when the schooner had slipped out eluding the espionage of the Sea Nymph. During that time the Hiaa's jib had pointed into a hundred inlets and lagoons searching for the sunken Beunaterran ship or a trace of her crew.

Prince, just on deck from below, glued a pair of glasses to his eyes. "If this isn't it," he told Cameron, "we'll tail back to Tahuata. Too much like a needle in a haystack. Everything going out—nothing coming in; we'll be busted flat."

The binoculars swept the water. "There's an opening," he said. "Probably a lagoon on the inside." The glasses continued the search. Suddenly they stopped, riveted on an object. He whistled. "Looks like the spars of a vessel—a steamer. Trucks just above water." He handed the glasses to Cameron. "We've found it," he said triumphantly. "Look! Half mile this side of the break. She tried for the entrance, hit the reef and slid off. Not more than ten feet of the spars above water."

After a long scrutiny, Cameron agreed that the spars were those of a steamer.

"We'll run in close and anchor," Prince said. "I'll take a whaleboat into the lagoon for a look around. This island according to the charts ought to be Temgui, but the charts aren't always right. If it's Temgui, the natives are a cross between Tahitan and Maori, ruled by their own chieftains. The island is nominally French with no resident whites. Sanchez spoke of fighting with them, but the directory says they are peaceful."

"Better take rifles," Cameron warned.

Prince nodded.

THE three hundred odd Temguians who lived, loved and laughed in the way of their ancestors in idyllic isolation had changed much since that day a year before when strange white men had swarmed down on their beaches and into their lagoon from a steamer which had crashed on the reef outside during a blow.

Met with the hospitality inherent in the Polynesian, the white men, although their skins were as dark as those of their hosts, had retaliated by appropriating the best huts, taking yams, breadfruit, taro and pigs without payment, and lastly, the women of the islanders who pleased their fancy.

The Temguians could not understand such behaviour. White men rarely visited their island, but those who did—traders, were halfway decent.

But even a worm will turn under continued provocation. The Temguians had finally chased the white men who had no guns, into the far corners of the island, exterminating them to the man, all except one, the leader, who had escaped in a leaky dugout.

When Prince's whaleboat, sounding as it came, entered the lagoon and grounded on the beach below the village, it was met with sullen silence. A few very old men were there, but the others had gone into the bush on word that a strange boat had been sighted.

"Iorana," Prince called in greeting to an old graybeard who watched the whaleboat suspiciously.

"Iorana," the patriarch returned without warmth.

Speaking in Tahitan, Prince asked where the people were.

"They have gone into the hills. They have no liking for you. White men are devils!"

Little by little, Prince got the story. And under his civil questioning, the old man visibly thawed out. Prince, he saw, was not the same breed as those from the wrecked ship.

"I will send word to the chief," the

old man finally said. "I will tell him that you are not as other white devils. Meanwhile it is better that you stay on your ship."

"DEPTH and width in the passage," Prince told Cameron, "and good holding ground at nine fathoms inside. In case of weather we can get through without trouble. Now for a look at the wreck. Break out the diving gear."

Two hours later, Prince encased in a diving suit was on the ocean's floor alongside the foundered steamer. That it was the vessel he sought was evidenced by the name on the overhang of the fantail which was tilted upward at an angle which allowed a purply twilight to fall on it. The name of the vessel was Santo Marcos and her registry, Monterrey, capital of Beunaterra. He climbed aboard.

Pulling his air hose and life line after him cautiously—the old vessel's bulwarks were rough—he entered the cabin, throwing a beam from his waterproof flashlight before him.

Where would a Latin American presidente, running away from a revolution, carry a large sum of money? Prince asked himself the question and promptly answered it. Where he could watch it. Not in the ship's strong box, but in his own cabin.

A passageway led for'ard. On each side were staterooms. The door of the second was locked. Prince smashed it with an axe from a rack on the wall and entered. Ranged against the wall opposite the bunk was a tier of small boxes. He lifted one. The weight of the box told the story.

Lugging it with him he returned to deck, cleared his lines and signalled to be taken up.

Back on the Hiaa, with helmet off, he watched Cameron break open the box. The contents were twenty-dollar American gold pieces.

THE next day was the greatest the Hiaa had ever known. From early morn till noon, Prince, Cameron and the Rappa bosun took turns below. And one by one the boxes came up. Not all contained American gold pieces. Some were filled with the coin of a half dozen different nationalities, both silver and gold. One box contained English pennies.

"Carlos Sanchez must have salted down everything in sight," Prince said as he nailed the lid back on. "How does the total stack up?"

Cameron figured with a lead pencil on the back of an envelope. "One hundred and ninety-three thousand, not counting the silver and the pennies," he reported.

Prince nodded. "Clean as a whistle. Tomorrow we'll take a look at the strong box and the other staterooms."

But he counted without the weather. About the middle of the afternoon, came a heavy downpour of rain followed by big wind squalls. The sky turned a lurid copper. It was evident that something was making.

Prince went below and looked at the barometer. It was at 29.85 and pumping. He returned to deck and surveyed the entrance to the lagoon.

"We ought to be inside," he said.

"Big weather, he come, I think," said the Rappa bosun.

Cameron nodded. "Yeah, looks like hurricane weather."

"Get up the hooks," Prince ordered, "and we'll go in. We'll tow a whaleboat astern against back draughts. I think we can make the lagoon without warping."

Two hours later the Hiaa was inside, anchored a quarter of a mile offshore. And not a bit too soon. The coppery, cloud mussed sky turned to deep indigo and a sixty-mile wind hurled a line of booming surf on the beach outside.

Before the Hiaa had snugged down

MIDWEST..
FACTORY·TO·YOU
SAVES 50%

ZIP!
and your STATION FLASHES IN

HALF the Cost... TWICE the Performance
14 TUBES FOR THE PRICE OF 8

This great new Midwest has caught the nation's fancy, because scores of marvelous new features like Dial-A-Matic Tuning*, Electrik-Saver* (optional*) give magnificent world-wide reception and glorious crystal clear realism. America OK's Midwest radios because they out-perform ordinary sets on a point-for-point comparison. Not a cut-price set, but a more powerful super performing radio in a big, exquisitely designed cabinet

of matched walnut! You are triply protected with Foreign Reception Guarantee . . . One-Year Warranty and Money-Back Guarantee. Now, you can roam the world in a flash . . . switching instantly from American programs to police, amateur, commercial, airplane and ship broadcasts ... to the most fascinating foreign programs. When you buy the Midwest factory-to-you way, you deal directly with the factory that makes radios — instead of paying extra profits to wholesalers, distributors, retailers, etc.

only
$39.95 BUYS
A NEW
1937 WORLD WIDE
MIDWEST

Your radio dollar goes twice as far when you buy a MIDWEST!

Send for FREE 40-PAGE CATALOG!
Remember! Nothing of value is added to a radio just because it is handled many times. You have a year to pay . . . terms as low as 10c a day . . . . you secure the privilege of 30 days FREE trial in your own home.

ZIP!... and Your Station Flashes In!
Your radio enjoyment is doubled with Dial-A-Matic Tuning, the amazing new Midwest feature that makes this radio practically tune itself. Zip!.. Zip!... Zip! ... stations come in instantly, automatically, perfectly . . . as fast as you can push buttons.

30 DAYS FREE TRIAL!

For seventeen years, Midwest engineers have pioneered many features and advantages which others quickly copied. The new 1937 Midwest is designed years in advance. It has everything! Not just two or three outstanding features, but scores of new developments...many of them exclusive. Send for the FREE 40-page book. See for yourself that Midwest offers today's greatest radio values. See why so many say: "Midwest sets the pace!"

Midwest engineers discussing new chassis

MIDWEST RADIO CORP.
DEPT. K-27
Established 1920
CINCINNATI, OHIO, U.S.A.
Cable Address MIRACO...All Codes

PASTE COUPON ON 1c POSTCARD...OR WRITE TODAY!

MIDWEST RADIO CORPORATION
Dept. K-27, Cincinnati, O.
Send me your new FREE catalog and complete details of your liberal 30-day FREE trial offer.
(Special offer and prices prevail only when dealing direct with factory by mail.)

Name
Address
Town   State
User-Agents Make Easy Extra Money   Check Here ☐ for details.

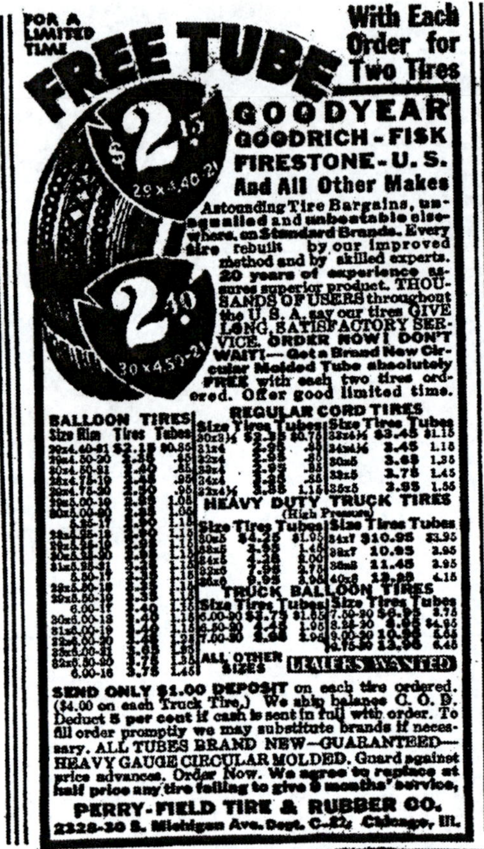

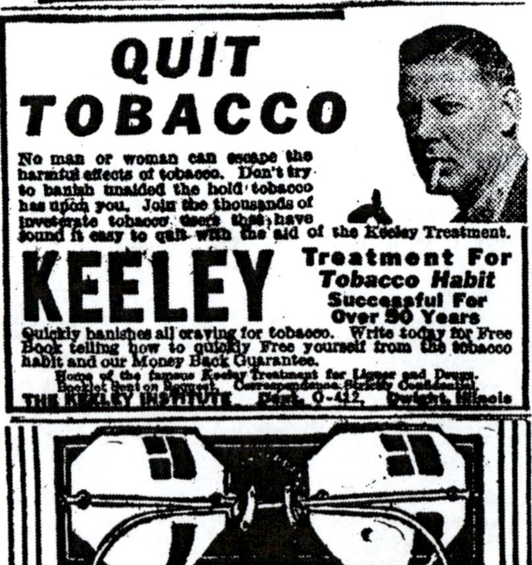

against the sea kicking up the lagoon, a white schooner yacht, heeling till her copper showed, scudded through the entrance. With a man heaving a lead in her bows, she skimmed over the water and dropped anchor two hundred yards from the Hiaa. It was the Sea Nymph.

HALF an hour after her chain had rattled in her hawse pipe, a boat swung over and headed for the Hiaa.

"Turlock's making a call," he said to Cameron, "and by the bulk of the fellow he's got with him, I'd say it was Thompson." He was right.

Turlock shook the rain drops from his oilskin. "Well," he said, addressing Prince, "ripper outside. Nice snug anchorage here. I'm Bill Turlock——" He stopped short, his eyes on the tier of boxes on the poop.

Prince damned himself for not getting the stuff out of sight.

"Been doing a little salvaging!" Turlock grunted, his eyes slitting. He nodded slightly to Thompson and turned on Prince. "That's what we came to see you about. I've bought an interest in Thompson's interest if you know what I mean. Two hundred thousand dollars. And seeing that I paid out good money, I've been clawing around these islands trying to locate a damned double crossing skunk by the name of Prince who froze out his mate! Back!" he snarled as Prince sprang forward, "or I'll blow your head off!" A hand came from beneath his slicker and in it was an automatic.

Surprised, totally unprepared, Prince gazed from Turlock to Thompson who held a Colt on Cameron. Prince had never suspected that Turlock would resort to open piracy. He'd imagined that scheming and underhandedness would be Turlock's tactics in trying for a share of the Santo Marco's loot.

He gauged the distance to Turlock, meanwhile trying to get Cameron's eye.

don't Worry about Rupture

● Why put up with days . . . months . . . YEARS of discomfort, worry and fear? Learn now about this perfected invention for all forms of reducible rupture. Surely you keenly desire—you eagerly CRAVE to enjoy life's normal activities and pleasures once again. To work . . . to play . . . to live . . . to love . . . with the haunting Fear of Rupture banished from your thoughts! Literally *thousands* of rupture sufferers have entered this *Kingdom of Paradise Regained*. Why not you? Some wise man said, "Nothing is impossible in this world"—and it is true, for where others fail is where we have had our greatest success in many cases! Even doctors—thousands of them—have ordered for themselves and their patients. Unless your case is absolutely hopeless, *do not despair*. The coupon below brings our Free Rupture Book in plain envelope. Send the coupon now.

Patented AIR-CUSHION Support Gives Nature a Chance to Close the OPENING

Think of it! Here's a surprising yet simple-acting invention that permits Nature to close the opening—that holds the rupture securely but gently, day and night, at work and at play! Thousands of grateful letters express heartfelt thanks for results beyond the expectation of the writers. What is this invention—How does it work? Will it help me? Get the complete, fascinating facts on the Brooks Automatic Air Cushion Appliance—send now for *free* Rupture Book.

Cheap - Sanitary - Comfortable

Rich or poor—ANYONE can afford to buy this remarkable, LOW-PRICED rupture invention! But look out for imitations and counterfeits. The Genuine Brooks is never sold in stores or by agents. Your Brooks is made up, after your order is received, to fit your particular case. You buy direct at the low "maker-to-user" price. The perfected Brooks is sanitary, light-weight, inconspicuous. Has no hard pads to gouge painfully into the flesh, no stiff, punishing springs, no metal girdle to rust or corrode. It brings heavenly comfort and security—while the Automatic Air Cushion continually works, in its own, unique way, *to help Nature get results!* Learn what this patented invention can mean to you—send coupon quick!

C. E. BROOKS,
Inventor

SENT ON TRIAL!

No . . . don't order a Brooks now—FIRST get the complete, revealing explanation of this world-famous rupture invention, THEN decide whether you want the comfort—the freedom from fear and worry—the security—the same amazing results thousands of men, women and children have reported. They found our invention the answer to their prayers! Why can't you? And you risk nothing as the complete Appliance is *sent on trial*. Surely you owe it to yourself to investigate this no-risk trial. Send for the facts now—today—hurry! All correspondence strictly confidential.

FREE! Latest Rupture Book Explains All!

Sent You In Plain Envelope Just Clip and Send Coupon ➞

Brooks Appliance Co., 209-J State St., Marshall, Mich.

PROOF!

Read These Reports on Reducible Rupture Cases.

(In our files at Marshall, Michigan, we have over 31,000 grateful letters which have come to us entirely unsolicited and without any sort of payment.)

Likes Brooks Best

"I bought one of your Rupture Appliances in 1933, wore it day and night for one year and laid it aside last December. The rupture hasn't bothered me since. I used several others without success until I got a Brooks."—J. B. McCarter, Route 2, Box 104, Oregon City, Ore.

"Runs and Plays"

"My son has not worn the Appliance for over a year. He wore one for ten years and I am very grateful now to think he has laid it aside. He is twelve years old, runs and plays hard like all boys and is never bothered about the rupture."—Mrs. M. George, Route 1, Box 103, Cumberland, Md.

Mail This Coupon NOW!

**BROOKS APPLIANCE CO.
209-J State St., Marshall, Mich.**

Without obligation, please send your FREE BOOK on Rupture, PROOF of Results, and TRIAL OFFER—all in plain envelope.

Name ....

Street ....

City .... State ......

State whether for Man ☐ Woman ☐ or Child ☐

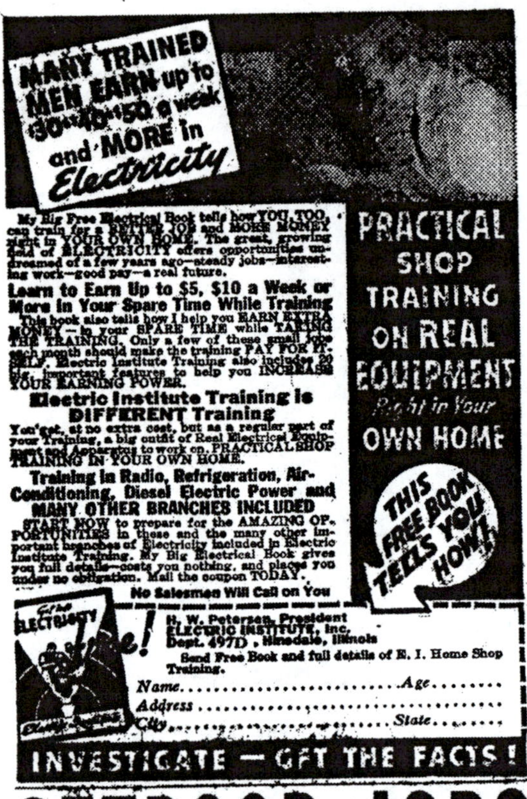

"How much—" Turlock began. Prince jumped.

The maneuver was disastrous. Turlock was not to be caught napping. He stepped to one side and smashed Prince over the head with the gun barrel. As the captain of the Hiaa went out, he heard the crash of Thompson's pistol.

WHEN Prince wakened he was in strange surroundings. The walls of a thatched hut stared at him and through the opening that served as a window he could see the branches of an avacado tree. It was early morning and Prince's head ached. He drew himself up from the pile of tapa mats and looked about.

On the opposite side of the hut, Cameron lay with a rag about his head. Outside, the howl of wind told that the gale was still blowing.

Then he became conscious of another person in the room: a broad shouldered, goldenskinned man with a magnificent chest sitting cross-legged by his side. His brown eyes were anxious.

"You are awake, Narri," the islander said in soft Tahitan; "when your men bring you ashore I think perhaps you and your mate both die— And I am very sorry."

"The schooner—my crew?" Prince asked.

"Schooner still in lagoon. Crew in village."

"You no remember me, Narri?" the islander asked. "I know you right away."

This was the second time the man had addressed Prince by a Polynesian name. Curiously, Prince looked at him. A picture floated out of the past. The picture of a wharf, an incoming steamer, diving boys, a dorsal fin, shreds of flesh between thigh and knee.

"I remember," Prince held out his hand.

"Many times have I thought of you,"

Narri said, clasping it warmly. "It seems, brother, that can repay some of that debt. I know not all that has happened, but from what your men told me, there are white devils out there," he pointed to the lagoon, "who have stolen your schooner and forced your crew ashore. I, Don-Prince, chief of the Temguians, will order my men to kill the white devils and restore my brother's ship."

"You have guns, brother?"

"No, but we have war clubs and fish spears."

"These men are bad—very bad," Prince warned. "They have guns and they will shoot. They will give their sailors guns and orders to shoot."

Narri shrugged his shoulders. "My brother didn't count the cost that day in Papeete. Nor shall I."

"We shall recapture the schooner," Prince agreed, "and we shall try to do it without loss of life. And this is the way."

Narri inclined his head. When Prince concluded, he nodded agreement.

Prince walked to the window and surveyed the two schooners and the lagoon. For the time being Turlock would have to stay inside. No craft in the world could get out over that foam lashed bar, let alone claw off if it did.

EARLY dusk two days later. The gale was fast dying and it was possible that Turlock might try to slip out. Whaleboats plying from the Hiaa to the Sea Nymph told that the Santo Marco's had been transhipped.

Prince stalked toward the canoe house to join Narri and thirty men armed with clubs and fish spears.

Orders from Narri and a large war canoe slipped into the water.

Driving between the schooners and the entrance, it veered sharply and with a keen-eyed Temguian in the bow, approached the Sea Nymph.

If the money had been transhipped, as it no doubt had been, Turlock and Thompson would be aboard the Sea Nymph, leaving the Hiaa deserted.

A whispered command from Narri and the paddlers rested. The canoe drifted. There were two splashes as Narri and Prince slipped into the water, unarmed except for sheath knives.

Silently they swam to the schooner. They rounded it and paddled aft. Prince's hand gripped the strake and he drew himself up to where he could peer over the rail. Narri followed.

A Kanaka with a rifle on his shoulder paced the poop. Amidships was another armed figure. Prince assumed another sentry was on the forepeak.

Lounging in a deck chair was an opaque bulk. A match flared, hands cupped it and lit a pipe. Turlock.

Prince and Narri slipped over the rail, ducked along the cabin and crept toward the Kanaka, Prince drawing a belaying pin as he passed it.

He raised the hardwood pin. He poised it. The sentry crossed the deck, looked into the darkness and turned. Crack! Narri caught the man and his gun before either had time to clatter to the deck. He eased the victim into the scuppers.

The bulk that was Turlock gave no indication that he had heard the thud of the belaying pin.

Prince threw the pin hard into the water. It splashed. Turlock rose from his chair and walked to the rail. Prince followed, treading softly. The sheath knife was in his hand.

Turlock stared into the darkness.

Apparently he made up his mind that the splash was a fish, for he grunted and stepped backward. Something hard, cold, sharp, pressed into the small of his back. A voice hissed a warning into his ear. He jerked, then was still. There was death in the voice.

"Six inches of steel, Turlock, in your gizzard if you blat! If you don't believe it, raise your voice. All right, Narri, tie him up."

With a coil of light line, the Temguian rapidly lashed the surprised Turlock. A handful of the same line was wadded up and thrust in his mouth. Making sure that the lashing was tight, Prince and Narri crept down the cabin companion. Thompson would be asleep below.

Darkness and unfamiliar surroundings made the descent slow. They traversed the cabin feeling along the walls for a passage to the staterooms when a loud yell broke out on deck. Turlock had spit out the gag.

With a bound Prince was on deck. Then up the companion sprinted a figure. It carried a ship's lantern in one hand and a pistol in the other. The light beams revealed Turlock. The lantern swung in an arc and the pistol blazed as Thompson saw Prince.

Prince ducked low and jumped. Again the pistol cracked, so near that the powder stung him.

Men were running from fora'ard: Kanakas, most of them armed. Prince threw himself at Thompson. A flailing fist struck, the pistol clattered to the deck and the two men clinched. As they went down, a voice roared orders into the darkness. Narri, calling on his men to board the schooner.

Prince seized a handhold on Thompson's tousled hair. He banged his head into the deck. Another terrific bang and the man went limp. As Prince arose, ship's lights flared out, revealing a group of disarmed Kanakas surrounded by triumphant Temguians. The Sea Nymph had been captured.

THE Hiaa was getting ready to put to sea. Thompson and Turlock were in irons below. They would be turned over to the French at Papeete and unless Prince missed his guess, they would be welcome. The goods were on Turlock at last. Thompson was an accessory. Noumea for both—and for how long depended on the temper of the provincial judge. As for the Sea Nymph, she'd have to stay in the Temguian lagoon till the French admiralty disposed of her.

The money had been divided and to make it clear, set aside in three piles. Prince explained it to Narri.

"This," he said, touching one pile, "is for pickanniny in Valparaiso, this," touching another, "is for me and my men. This," touching the third, "is for Temgui. I place it to your credit in bank at Papeete, then I make voyage back here with cloth, rifles, steel fish hooks, axes, needles, thread and cotton. And if Donprince will go into his canoe, we will hoist our sails."

The Hiaa slipped out with the tide. On the headland above the entrance to the lagoon, stood a golden skinned man with magnificent shoulders. He waved at the figures on the schooner's deck. They waved back.

He turned to the graybeard, the same one to whom Prince had first talked. "Never was such a white one," he said. "My brother, Narri."

"Aie," the old one agreed. "Never was such a white one."

Printed in the United States
138192LV00003B/14/A